RICHER BY FAR

RICHER BY FAR

•

Elizabeth C. Main

AVALON BOOKS
THOMAS BOUREGY AND COMPANY, INC.
401 LAFAYETTE STREET
NEW YORK, NEW YORK 10003

PRINTED IN THE UNITED STATES OF AMERICA
ON ACID-FREE PAPER
BY HADDON CRAFTSMEN, BLOOMSBURG, PENNSYLVANIA

To my family. Thanks for all your help. Your constant encouragement has meant everything to me. Thanks also to Helen Vandervort, my reading partner, for reading and critiquing the manuscript through all its many revisions.

Chapter One

Tory tossed the cellular phone to the passenger seat of the yellow convertible in disgust. She'd already left two messages on Carson's machine and didn't feel like suffering through his excessively cute answering machine routine again. It started with Carson doing a bad imitation of Humphrey Bogart, ''Here's listening to you, kid!'' and went downhill from there. She fumbled two extra-strength Excedrin from her bag and swallowed them dry. Her head had been pounding all morning and the two tablets she had taken earlier hadn't touched the pain. After having rushed to her office early to put the finishing touches on a new customer's investment portfolio, she had flown to central Oregon to deal with an inheritance from her uncle, so her day was pretty well shot—and it was just past noon.

She returned her attention to the road ahead just in time to slam on her brakes. A brown cow with a white

1

face straddled the center line, or what would have been the line if this godforsaken highway had possessed one. Trying to avoid the barbed-wire fences bracketing the narrow road, Tory twisted the wheel sharply until she brought the rented convertible to a sliding stop just inches from the unmoving animal. "Stupid cow!" she shouted into the country silence.

For two cents, she'd turn the car around right here and head back to civilization, or what passed for civilization in Oregon. This couldn't possibly be the right road, and even if it were, she wouldn't want to visit any town at the end of it. Her list of complaints was growing, starting with the primitive conditions at the High Desert Airport: no skycaps, no Starbucks, no one at the desk when she tried to pick up her rental car. She didn't even want to think about the slow-moving clerk who finally emerged from the back room, his lunch napkin tucked into his collar. He kept shaking his head about the Buick Skylark she thought she had reserved, but when he finally realized that she needed to get to Silver Pine for an appointment, he hastily commandeered his teenage son's '67 Mustang convertible for her. She should have taken Carson up on his offer to fly her down here today. So far, everything had taken twice as long as seemed reasonable.

And now this stupid cow. She pounded on the horn. The enormous animal gave out a bellow that shook the crows loose from the fence posts. "Yeah, I agree," Tory answered. "Life's a bummer. Now move!" The cow looked at her and bellowed again.

"Get out of here!" Tory yelled, standing up in the seat as best she could. "Go on, move it!" Another blast on the horn scattered the crows once more, but made no visible impact on the cow.

"Oh, for Pete's sake," Tory muttered, flinging open the door and stepping out onto the dusty roadbed. Her Etienne Aigner flats blended nicely into the dust. She kept the door between her and the animal as she waved her arms. "Shoo! Shoo!" If the road were a little wider, she could go around, but she was facing the broadest cow imaginable.

As though responding to an invitation, the cow lumbered toward her, causing her to retreat to the front seat and slam the door. Just then she heard the roar of an engine and spotted a battered white pickup truck approaching from the rear. She stood up and waved her arms furiously overhead until she was certain the truck was stopping.

The driver uncoiled his length from the front seat and emerged from the cab. Under the brim of his cowboy hat she could see a shadow of dark beard and a very square jaw. She prepared a dazzling smile, tilting her head up at him, but he didn't even glance at her. He was looking at the cow, and he was mad.

"What did you do to her?"

"Me? I didn't do any—"

"You didn't hit her?"

"What kind of silly question is that? No, I didn't hit her, but I sure tried hard," she shot back.

"Look, lady, this is open-range country. You're supposed to watch out for her, not the other way around."

"Well, pardon me for driving on *her* road. What on earth was I thinking?" She dropped back into the driver's seat, slammed the gearshift into position, and ground the starter until the powerful engine roared to life. "Now, if you'll just get Bossy out of the way, I'll be going. Nice of you to ask how I am."

She revved the motor as the tall stranger approached the cow and put a gentle hand on her flank to guide her aside. The moment they moved far enough out of the way, Tory gunned the car forward and past them. Tossing her chestnut hair, she permitted herself one backward glance in the mirror to make sure they were both covered with dust before she sped down the road toward Silver Pine and her inheritance.

The attorney's letter had instructed Tory to take State Highway 17 south from the airport until just past the irrigation canal. There, she was to turn right onto Fremont Road, which skirted Silver Pine and would take her right by her house. The letter had gone on to say that she "couldn't possibly miss the house, the only three-story place for at least a hundred miles." Moments later, Tory stared in amazement at the fairy-tale structure that appeared before her. Through the orderly row of aspens flanking the overgrown driveway, she could see that the house—no, not just a house, a mansion—rose up and up, ending in a rounded turret that should have had Rapunzel standing at one of the curved windows. Accustomed as she was to the sleek black-and-white decor of her Seattle penthouse, Tory felt she had detoured into another century.

The cool delft blue of the siding was accented by white trim surrounding the elongated rectangular windows. Burgundy sashes further highlighted the windows, and all three colors were repeated in a geometric design that graced the top of each of the three stories, as well as the turret.

A deep, covered porch surrounded the house, and the graceful spindles of a colorful railing ended in pillars flanking the broad front steps leading to the front door beyond. And what a door. Even from this distance she could discern the ornate carving on its lower wooden panels. The upper part of the door was split by two long, thin rectangles of glass surrounded by more intricately carved woodwork.

The attorney had badly understated the beauty of the house. His comments about it being a "three-story place" didn't begin to cover it, and Tory quickly revised her financial estimate of the value of her uncle's house upward. Before seeing it, she had assumed that her inheritance consisted of some kind of ramshackle country farmhouse, probably with a chicken shed out back. But this . . . this was something else. No wonder she'd already received a firm offer from the California Development Corporation. When she'd been sitting in Seattle, fuming over the need to come all the way down here to settle the paperwork on the property, their offer had seemed more than generous, but now that she'd seen the house, she determined that they'd have to come up with quite a bit more money before she'd agree to complete the sale. Too bad the property was in such an out-of-the-way place. It would fetch a lot more in a decent location.

Up close, however, neglect of the property was apparent. Along one side of the house, weeds had long since taken over what seemed to have been a formal rose garden. A fragrant honeysuckle vine dripped off the wraparound porch, while huge lilac bushes and unpruned roses all but obscured most of the front windows. The paint was starting to peel from the pillars and the front steps, and unswept leaves littered the porch, trapped by the spindles of the railing.

Tory shut off the engine and was engulfed in a silence broken only by the singing of birds. A large golden dog sprawled on the old-fashioned porch. According to the letter, Mrs. Rafferty from next door—wherever that was—would be over to show her through the house at one o'clock. Tory checked the Gucci bracelet watch Carson had given her last Christmas. It was already after one, and she hoped Mrs. Rafferty wouldn't be long. Tory just wanted to get this over with and catch the late flight back to Seattle.

She approached the front steps, keeping a wary eye on the dog. "Good dog," she said uncertainly, as she put one foot on the bottom step. She didn't know much about dogs. Her father had never allowed her to have one and she was uncomfortable around them. Her only experience with animals, other than the cow today, was a kitten she had befriended on the way home from third grade. Her father had been away on business and Tory had enjoyed three full days playing with the innocent little ball of fluff. Upon his return, however, there were harsh words between him and her mother, and the kitten was sent to live elsewhere. The dog on the porch raised his head and watched her with an inquisitive expression for a while before scrambling to his feet. She hurriedly returned to the car for the cell phone, muttering, "What is it with the animals in this place?"

Information gave her the numbers for two Raffertys in Silver Pine. Sarah Rafferty's phone rang and rang with no answer. The other number was a veterinarian's office, and the cheerful receptionist, who identified herself as Cindy, said the doctor was out on a call. However, she volunteered that "Brian's aunt should be around somewhere because she's supposed to meet Jim's niece from Seattle. Hey, that's you, I bet."

Tory stifled her initial sarcastic reply and concentrated on the task at hand. "That's right. Unfortunately, Mrs. Rafferty doesn't seem to be anywhere around."

"That's funny. Well, did you try the door? It's probably open."

"Open? But the house has been empty since my uncle died—"

"Give it a try, okay? Nobody locks things up much around here." Cindy raised her voice over the background sound of barking dogs. "Call back if you can't get in. Sarah's probably on her way over right now."

Next, Tory dialed the lawyer's number and got the same story from his receptionist, who sounded almost as cheerful as Cindy. Must be something in the water here, she thought. Her own secretary was efficient and pleasant, but Tory wouldn't describe her as cheerful.

"Wasn't Sarah supposed to meet you there?"

How did anyone have a private life in this town? No wonder her father had left right after his high school graduation. It was like living in a fishbowl. "Yes, but she isn't here."

"Try the door. Maybe she left a note inside."

"Inside?" she asked, knowing the response it would bring. It came right on cue.

"Nobody locks doors around here."

"So I've heard. When do you expect Mr. Thorne?"

"Shouldn't be too long now. He went over to have lunch with his parents, the way he does every Friday, regular as anything. He used to be in partnership with his dad—his dad's the other part of Thorne and

Thorne—so Don goes over once a week for lunch and to talk about business. Makes his dad feel good that Don consults him, even though he's retired.''

I knew it, Tory thought. *Hometown boy falls into local law firm and never leaves.* With the sluggish pace of Silver Pine, she couldn't imagine that there would be much legal business to discuss each week, but maybe that would work in her favor. If the Thorne family lunch hour was based on talk about the firm's clients, it shouldn't last too long. ''Will he be coming back to the office then?'' she inquired.

''Well, he's supposed to get a haircut, but he'll probably come here right after that.''

''Probably?''

She laughed. ''I'm sure he'll be here soon as he can.''

''Please tell him that I'll be there at two o'clock as scheduled, and I have a plane to catch later, so I won't have extra time to wait.'' For the second time today Tory tossed the phone. This wasn't her day for productive calls, but then she wasn't used to dealing with small-town inefficiency. She had no idea about the haircut appointments and family lunches among the people in Seattle with whom she did business, and she was glad she didn't normally have to deal with such trivialities. Her attorney in Seattle didn't wander off in the middle of the day to have lunch with his parents—assuming he had parents—and if he did, she'd never hear about it, or them, thank goodness. She drummed her fingers on the hot steering wheel and tried to ignore the continuing throb of her headache.

Minutes later, though it seemed to her like hours, Tory could make out a petite figure with silver hair swept up into a loose knot atop her head hurrying up the driveway, a glass pitcher in one hand and a covered pan in the other. The elusive Sarah Rafferty, Tory thought.

''I had to come the long way around,'' she announced from thirty feet away. ''Couldn't jump the ditch with this armload . . . and besides, I couldn't leave till the apple cake came out of the oven. You do like apple cake, don't you?'' She started up the steps with Tory close behind. ''I wanted to make some lemonade—and then at first I couldn't find the pitcher because I'd left it outside when I watered the tomatoes. Oh, I should have brought you some tomatoes, but I assumed you'd go on in the house anyway and not stand out here in the hot sun, especially with your complexion. You don't want to ruin that lovely skin. . . . ''

She paused for breath and handed Tory the pitcher, in the process freeing one hand to open the unlocked front door. The dog wagged his tail hopefully.

''I wondered where he'd gotten to. He keeps showing up here. . . . No, Jake, you stay outside.''

Tory edged past the dog and followed Mrs. Rafferty inside, closing the door firmly behind her. A quick glance at the entryway gave Tory the same impression of elegance overlaid with neglect as the outside had. The deep red and blue of an Oriental rug harmonized with the mellow tones of hardwood floors and extensive paneling, and an ornate vase filled with feathers stood on the floor beside a carved chest that functioned as a telephone table. The sunlight that filtered through sheer window curtains revealed a thick layer of dust over everything, and a spider had spun a web across the feathers in the vase. Why would someone have built such a magnificent house, and then let it go to ruin like this? It was creepy, and rather sad. Besides, even though the place had an abandoned air, it should have been locked up after her uncle died. If this was the way the local lawyer took care of her property, she was lucky she still had an inheritance to sell. "Look, Mrs. Rafferty—"

"Call me Sarah." Sarah turned and formally extended the fragrant apple cake to Tory. "Welcome to Silver Pine. We all hope you're going to enjoy it here."

Tory tried again. "Look, Mrs. Rafferty . . . Sarah . . . this is all very kind of you, but I won't be staying in Silver Pine. I just came to sign some papers." She handed back the cake pan.

"Oh, I was afraid of that, but we were hoping . . ." Sarah suddenly looked stricken. "Where are my manners? I haven't even told you how sorry we all were when your uncle died. Jim was such—"

Tory put up a restraining hand. "I didn't know him at all. Our family was never close, and this house came as a complete surprise to me. I didn't even know where Silver Pine was."

Sarah carried the cake pan thoughtfully toward the kitchen. "Well, I'm sorry you didn't get a chance to know him. He was the best neighbor anyone ever had, and he loved my apple cake. That's what made me think of bringing you some today." Sarah rummaged in the cupboard for plates and glasses as she spoke.

"Yes, well, I'm sure it's very good. Thank you for the thought, but you'll have to take the rest of it back. I have to catch a plane for Seattle later."

"Tonight? But—"

"As I think I just explained, I can't stay." She didn't add that the idea of staying in this dusty old place gave her the willies, but Sarah must have recognized the look on her face.

"Don't think the house always looked like this." Sarah ran her index finger through the dust coating the chest that held the telephone. "It used to be quite a showplace, with all of Jim's carvings and the antiques they'd collected and such. After Ellen died—two years ago in March, it was—well, Jim didn't seem to care so much about it. He put all his energy into community projects instead, just didn't feel like being here anymore. And then, of course, it's been closed up completely for the last month. I cleaned up the master bedroom for you, and I did the bathrooms, of course. Didn't do as much of the house as I'd planned, but you can tell where I went by following the footprints in the dust." She smiled at Tory. "We'd hoped some nice young family would move in. The trees between here and the river make such a good park for children to play in. Do you have children?" Tory shook her head, so Sarah continued, "Well, don't worry. You will someday. When our kids left— Jim and Ellen never had any of their own, you know—it got mighty quiet around here, I'll tell you. Mighty quiet."

Not quiet enough, Tory thought. Would this woman ever run down? She took a tiny bite of the warm apple cake and murmured appreciatively. It tasted of cinnamon and butter, not exactly her typical afternoon snack, which ran more to rice cakes and Diet Coke.

"Here. Try your lemonade," Sarah said, handing her a glass. "The secret is to squeeze the lemons fresh. They say frozen is just as good, but this is much better. I grow my own mint too. Can you taste it?"

Before Tory could reply, the thud of boots sounded on the porch, accompanied by a deep voice calling, "Aunt Sarah? You there?"

"Oh, that's my nephew, Brian. He wanted to meet you today. In fact, I'm surprised that he didn't get here before I did."

The doorway was suddenly filled with broad shoulders, shoulders that Tory recognized before she could even make out the face in the gloom of the front hall.

"Brian, come on in and meet Tory Baxter—" Sarah stared at his blood-covered hands and arms. "Brian, what happened?"

"Tory Baxter?" he said slowly, looking at Tory incredulously. *"You're* Jim's niece?"

"Brian, what happened?" repeated Sarah. "Are you all right?"

Something that might have passed for a smile crossed Brian's filthy face. "I'm fine, and so is Peterson's cow and her brand-new calf. That's why I'm late. Coming back from Barkers' place, I stopped to deliver the calf. Maybe Ms. Baxter already told you about it, seeing as how she so graciously stopped to help me."

"My goodness, in that silk blouse? And you never said a word." Sarah beamed from one to the other. "And the calf's all right, you say? Isn't that nice. Now, Brian, go wash up and you can have some cake and lemonade with us."

Tory found her voice at last. "I, uh, I think I'd better be getting into town to see Mr. Thorne. We have to sign some papers—"

"Yes, by all means. Let's not detain Ms. Baxter further," Brian said, ostentatiously holding the heavy door wide for her. "She has a very busy schedule and we certainly don't want to interrupt it with our quaint country customs."

Sarah gawked at her nephew, then turned in confusion to see Tory's scarlet face. "What on earth—"

"Thanks again for the cake, Sarah," Tory said, thrusting plate and glass at her. "It was wonderful."

Brian addressed the dog on the porch. "Better get out of the way, Jake, if you value your life."

"*Such* a pleasure to see you again, Dr. Rafferty." With as much dignity as she could muster, Tory stepped over Jake and marched to her car.

Shortly before two o'clock, Tory slid the convertible into a diagonal parking slot outside the law offices of Thorne & Thorne. At least there was no problem about traffic or parking on the main street—few cars and not a parking meter in sight. Bright baskets of red and white petunias adorned the antique light poles above the red-brick sidewalks. She read with amusement the poster affixed to the glass door in front of her, proudly announcing the upcoming Forty-eighth Annual Fourth of July Silver Pine Pet Parade. Forty-eight years of watching animals walk down the main street of town. What an exciting place. Maybe the cow she'd met would be the queen of the parade.

A middle-aged receptionist wearing a hairstyle not recently seen in Seattle looked up and smiled at the sound of the door opening. Unexpectedly, she raised her voice and announced over her shoulder, "Don, she's here." Apparently, intercoms hadn't yet made it to Silver Pine.

Like magic, a man shaped like Humpty Dumpty appeared from an inner office, attempting to shrug his way into a sports jacket and extend his hand in welcome simultaneously. The newly shaved sides of his head testified to the fact that he had, indeed, stopped for a haircut on his way back from lunch. "Hello, hello, Ms. Baxter. Don Thorne. Glad you made it okay. Jean, do we have any coffee left? Or maybe you'd like something cold."

"No, I'm fine . . . nothing, thanks," Tory replied as they shook hands. "I'm in a bit of a hurry—"

"Right, right. Let's just get started then." He waved her cheerfully into his private office and seated her in a massive green brocade–upholstered chair before settling himself behind his own cluttered mahogany desk. "How do you like Silver Pine so far? A bit smaller than Seattle." He chuckled at his own joke.

"A lot smaller. It's very nice, but . . ." She waited until he got the hint.

"Of course, of course. You're in a hurry, not here to chat. Now let me see. . . ." Putting on a pair of reading glasses, he shuffled through several files on his desk.

Jean's amused voice floated in from the front office. "On top of the filing cabinet."

He stood and retrieved the file. "Thanks, Jean. Of course, of course. I was looking at it earlier." His jovial manner changed as he whipped off his glasses and continued, "You know, Jim was a good friend of mine. Terrible shock when he went so fast. Terrible shock."

"Thank you, but—"

"We went to school together right down the street— your father, too. Did you see the school when you drove in? Big gray building?"

"No, I wasn't really looking—"

He dropped the file on the desk and picked up a slim white volume. "We went all through high school there. Everyone together, so you really got to know people— even the younger kids, like your dad. I dug out the annual from Jim's and my senior year to show you—

course your dad was just a freshman then." Dark blue letters spelled out SPHS 1949 against the white background of the yearbook in his hand. He flipped through the pages until he found the senior class pictures, then pointed to a smiling, handsome young man. "There's your uncle Jim. He always did take a good picture." He turned back a few pages to show her the freshman class picture. "And there's your dad. They looked a lot alike, didn't they? Your dad wasn't much for smiling though."

Tory barely glanced at the somber picture of her father. "No, he wasn't." She hurried on before Mr. Thorne could lose himself in more pictures of the good old days at SPHS 1949. "Maybe I could look at these some other time? I do need to get going—"

He reluctantly put aside the well-worn book and opened the file again. "You're right, of course, but we sure did have fun back then. Let's see, if we skip all the whereases and wherefores, it boils down to this, you get the house and the land fronting the river—in spite of, well, I guess you know about the problems Jim and your father had—"

"Problems?"

"Doesn't matter now, of course, with both of them gone—"

"My father never talked much about his brother, or Silver Pine, or any problems between them, and frankly, it seems irrelevant to me at this late date—"

"Probably so—"

"Look, I don't mean to be rude, but I really do have a time crunch." She checked her watch. "I have another meeting scheduled this afternoon and I need to get things finished up here so I can get back to Seattle on the late flight tonight."

His face clouded. "Oh, I see. I hadn't realized from your letter . . . I mean, I assumed you were coming to take possession—"

"Possession?" She laughed. "I run a very successful business in Seattle. What on earth would I do with a house in Silver Pine?"

"Yes, I see . . . well, we were just hoping to keep this property in the family, so to speak. So many changes around here with that NorthPointe business up on the hill and everything . . . and Jim and Ellen loved the place. You know how Ellen was about her home—"

"I'm afraid I don't. I never met either of them. My father didn't correspond at all with his brother—and I don't know whether he ever met Ellen."

"You're joking, of course. Surely you've—" He stopped in sudden embarrassment, then resumed briskly when she didn't answer. "As you say, it's ancient history. Certainly not worth mentioning at this late date. Now, let's look at the specifics." He resettled his glasses. "Other than some token bequests to various friends and neighbors, you are the sole heir to the house and property. But you should know that very little money goes with the house. Jim bequeathed all his money to the High Desert Land Trust. You're familiar with that?"

"Not really. Sort of an organized do-gooder outfit, I presume?"

"Well, I guess you could describe it that way. They buy private land for public benefit and they've been working to buy up as much land around town as they can. Ever since Ellen died, Jim has put most of his time and effort into that project, along with his city council work, of course. If you want to get poetic about it, maybe it's fair to say that her death made the present so much less interesting to him that he started working on the future instead—his community's future anyway. Jim's money is more than welcome to the group, but we're sure sorry to lose him around here.''

Tory could see his eyes starting to fill with tears and she shifted uncomfortably in her chair as he reached for a handkerchief from his back pocket. Don Thorne was not only a philosopher-lawyer, but one who couldn't seem to separate business from friendship. She'd be glad to get back to Seattle, where people kept their personal lives at home and let her get on with business efficiently.

Putting his handkerchief away, the lawyer continued. ''I might as well tell you straight out. Frankly, some of us were hoping that Jim would leave the house and land to the land trust—or to the town of Silver Pine itself, maybe for a park or something. But Jim made it clear that this house was to go to his family—to you, that is. He was mighty insistent, and who can blame him? Beautiful place like that, anybody'd want kin to have it. As kids, we spent plenty of time running around out there. Even climbed some of those pines when they were a lot smaller. Didn't do the trees much good, and my mother howled plenty about the pitch on my pants, but it was a wonderful place to play.'' He patted his ample waistline. ''Hard to imagine me climbing a tree, but I was a regular monkey way back when. So many memories . . .''

''Yes, I'm sure . . . but you'll no doubt agree that memories don't make money. Were you aware that my father founded the Northwest Financial Management Group?'' She extracted an embossed card from a monogrammed silver case and slid it across the desk. The heavy initials NFM stood out in bold relief across the top.

"I assure you that if my uncle had asked my father for his financial advice, he certainly wouldn't have recommended donating a big house like that, with trees and river frontage, to anybody. Not even in a town like this where property values are no doubt low. No offense, but I wouldn't recommend it either."

"If not a family home, it would have been a wonderful city park," he said sadly, "and some of us thought that the house would make a dandy museum."

"I'm sure it would have made a charming museum and park—but I'm a businesswoman, not the parks department."

Mr. Thorne sighed. "I see. Well, anyway, if you're not going to live there yourself, you'll still need a caretaker—"

"Mr. Thorne, I'm afraid you don't understand. I plan to sell the house."

"You do? Are you sure?" He brightened at the thought. "Well, then—"

"Of course I'm sure . . . and the sooner the better. I really don't have time to be running down here, as I told you."

"In that case, I'm sure that some of the people from the Silver Pine City Council would like a chance to talk to you, maybe put in a bid on behalf of the town—"

"That would be a waste of everyone's time, I think. You mentioned NorthPointe? That's a project of California Development, I believe? They've already been in touch with me—"

"Lind or Wright?"

"I beg your pardon?"

"You talked to Arlie Lind or Virgil Wright about this?"

"No, actually I talked to a Mr. Harper, from San Francisco. I don't know those other names."

"You will soon enough," he said glumly. "They're both on the city council. Arlie owns the Ford dealership here, and there are rumors around that Virgil's already been talking to California Development about selling a big piece of his ranch for that fancy ski resort they're planning to build. 'NorthPointe,' with an *e* on the end. Virgil and Arlie are all gung ho on everything to do with NorthPointe." He snorted. "You'd think they'd know better than to get involved in a project with a silly name like that."

"I don't understand. If these men are in favor of California Development's plans for my property, why would you want them to talk to me about city parks or whatever?"

"There are some others on the city council that don't exactly share their views on the way this town should grow. Those are the people I want you to talk to."

"I see. Well, I doubt that any public entity could match California Development's offer."

"Your choice, of course, but once you learn a few things about their plans—"

"Their plans are up to them," Tory said firmly. "Now, if you can help me with the necessary paperwork, I'm supposed to meet with Mr. Harper later this afternoon. He's flying in from San Francisco and I gave him your number as the best place to reach me."

"Just a minute." He raised his voice. "Jean?"

"On your desk, Don, probably under the yearbook."

"Oh, so it is. I got to looking at all those old pictures and missed it. Can you believe I was on the track team once? Pretty good sprinter, too." He started to pick up the yearbook again, but Tory just looked at him without comment until he got the hint and put it back down. "Yes, let's see. Here's the message. Uh-oh, looks like you have trouble." He read aloud, " 'Ms. Baxter: sorry, can't make it. Fever of a hundred and two. Meet Tuesday? Will call after doctor's appointment to confirm.' "

"Tuesday! I can't stay here until Tuesday."

"Sorry to contradict you, but it looks a little bit like you can't do anything else if you want to talk to this fellow, unless you want to make another trip down here."

"No, no. It would be better to settle this all at once. But I have so many things to do in Seattle."

"You can't do too much business over the long weekend anyway, can you?"

"Why not?"

"The Fourth of July—"

"Our clientele is international, Mr. Thorne, and very interested in making money. We don't stop much for holidays. Of course, I do have my laptop with me."

"Well, then, if you're going to stay . . . could I at least set up a meeting with some of the city council 'opposition party,' so to speak? We're not too formal in Silver Pine, so a meeting on Monday—say after the pet parade when everyone's in town anyway—wouldn't be much of a problem."

Everyone will be in town for the pet parade? How could she resist the lure of such an exciting prospect? "Well, I suppose—"

"Great! I know they'd appreciate at least having a chance to put their case forward."

"Okay, but tell them not to get their hopes up."

Chapter Two

As she emerged once again into the bright July sunshine of the street, Tory's view of her ridiculous yellow convertible was partially blocked by Brian's familiar tall form leaning against the hood. Once he saw her, Brian straightened and removed his straw hat, revealing a tangle of dark, curly hair.

"If I had a white flag, I'd wave it," he began.

"Meaning . . . ?" Tory's glacial tone offered no opening.

"Meaning we got off to kind of a bad start earlier—"

"You could call it that," Tory agreed.

"—and I'd like to rewind this film back a ways."

"Oh, you would? Back to before or after you accused me of . . . of attempting to *murder* a cow . . . just because I happened to be driving on a public road?"

He winced. "I vote for before. Yeah, way before that.

21

... Look, I didn't mean to accuse you, exactly. It just came out wrong—''

"Uh-huh—"

"—and I was worried about the cow."

"That was evident," she said, stepping around him and pulling open the car door.

"Truce?" he asked, giving her a tentative smile. His teeth were even and very, very white. He held out his large hand, palm up, over the car door between them.

After a small hesitation she said, "Oh, why not? Truce," placing her smaller hand in his. "Maybe I was a little abrupt myself." Their eyes met and, suddenly, they were laughing together. He held her hand a fraction of a second longer than necessary to seal the bargain, his hand warm and comforting. Unaccountably, Tory found herself disappointed when he released her.

After she climbed into the driver's seat, he closed the door firmly, but continued to rest his hands on the frame. "You'll be glad to know that Aunt Sarah gave me a verbal spanking after you left. Somehow, she got the funny idea I was a little rude to you back at the house."

"Imagine that." Tory was paying more attention to the way one of Brian's dark eyebrows rose than she was to his actual words.

"Seems she didn't think I welcomed you too well to Silver Pine. Anyway, she sent me to apologize—and to ask you to dinner tonight."

Tory tried to picture herself making conversation with Aunt Sarah. Maybe they could trade pickle recipes. "I have a lot of work to do—"

"On a Friday night?"

"This trip hasn't exactly fit into my schedule—"

"You have to eat dinner anyway."

"Really, I don't think—"

"Course it's only fair to warn you that I'll be there too. But I'll be on my best behavior, I promise."

Suddenly, Tory's work seemed less urgent to her, and after all, she had to eat somewhere. "How about your friend?" she asked.

"Friend . . . ?" There went the intriguing eyebrow again.

"You know . . . Bossy?"

"Sorry, just me, but I guarantee my table manners are better."

"Well, I do have to eat."

"My aunt's a great cook."

"Somehow I knew you were going to say that," she said, remembering the delicate apple cake.

"And she probably won't feed me unless you come too."

"Well, in that case, I'd better come. But first I have to find a place to stay and make some calls."

"Won't you be staying at the house? Aunt Sarah was over there this morning getting it ready for you."

Tory was doubtful. "You think so?"

"Why not? It's your house. Besides, it's handy to dinner. You won't have any trouble getting to Sarah's house. Take the long way around by road or just cut straight north through the trees and turn east at the biggest ponderosa. If you get to the river, you've gone too far."

"I can recognize a river when I see one, but I wouldn't know a ponderosa from a petunia."

"You're in luck. I know all about ponderosas—petunias too—so how about if I come get you . . . say about six?"

"That's really not necessary."

"Sure it is. You don't want to go through life not knowing a ponderosa from a petunia, do you? I'll give you the deluxe tour."

"Well, if it's the deluxe tour, okay."

"Say, isn't this Tim Bassett's Mustang? What's he doing renting it out . . . and on a Friday night? How's he going to be 'cool' without his wheels?"

"Don't ask me, ask his father. There was a mix-up at the airport and the Buick I reserved wasn't there. Guess I'll just have to be the cool one around town tonight."

"You'll be that, all right. No contest." Brian stepped back from the car, but continued to look intently at Tory. "See you at six."

Tory switched off the engine and craned her head to look all the way up at the turret standing guard over one corner of all three floors of her inheritance. Home, sweet castle, she thought, hoisting her fitted black Vuitton overnight case from the backseat of the convertible. She never flew anywhere without an emergency bag, not after that nightmare trip to Los Angeles a year ago that was supposed to last one afternoon, but had stretched into three long days.

She collected the cell phone and started up the front steps. Again, the sweet smell of honeysuckle wafted from the lacy green bushes that grew along each side of the porch columns. The retriever still sprawled across the doorway, but this time Tory tried to act confident as she stepped over him and opened the unlocked door, saying "Hello, Jake" as she passed. He thumped his tail and made as if to follow her inside, but she quickly closed the door. No animals in the house. That had been her father's rule for as long as she could remember. Animals just cluttered things up.

The late-afternoon sun slanted across the dusty hardwood floor, and the smell of apple cake lingered in the air. The cake was still on the kitchen counter. Sarah had left it, in spite of Tory's insistence that she wouldn't be back. Well, it had been a long time since her plastic-encased breakfast on the plane, and Sarah's moist cake had little in common with Horizon Air's version of a muffin anyway. She broke off a piece and savored its rich flavor as she dialed the San Francisco office of the ailing lawyer and talked to his apologetic secretary about rescheduling their appointment for next Tuesday at 1:00 P.M.

Then she tried Carson's number. She wondered for the umpteenth time whether it would be kinder of her to stay completely away from him, but he was good fun and she had tried to make it clear that their relationship wasn't going anywhere. She didn't have time for a serious relationship, and besides, he'd been around so long that she couldn't work up much excitement at the thought of him.

''Tory. It's about time.''

''Well, hello to you too.''

''Sorry. I just couldn't imagine what was taking you so long.''

''You weren't there when I called earlier,'' Tory said reasonably.

''Well, Gina came by and she wanted to go over the plans for the opening again.'' Carson's art gallery, Enjouement, was starting to attract some big names and he was constantly occupied with the promotion of its opening gala. Since Gina's father had provided a major source of funding for the gallery, Gina, an intense young artist with minimal talent, had only to suggest a meeting and Carson was available. "We tried out Le Chat Sceptique for lunch." The upscale new French restaurant was next door to his art gallery, and Carson was hoping that the two similarly named establishments would help each other by attracting some of the same people.

"How was it?"

"Pretty good. Pricey . . . elegant. Their hors d'oeuvres were spectacular, especially the *aubergines farcies duxelles*. In fact, Gina suggested we do a dual promotion with the restaurant for the gala. I like the idea. By the way, Gina said to say hello."

There was a slight pause. Tory knew Carson was hoping that the mention of Gina would make her jealous. Apparently, he hadn't quite given up hope that Tory's feelings for him would change. "I'll bet. And was she just devastated that I was out of town and couldn't join you for lunch?" Tory was at the bottom of Gina's list of favorite people, and that was fine with her. "Look, Carson, I'm stuck in Silver Pine this weekend."

"The whole weekend? What can you find to do there for an entire weekend?"

"I'll have you know that, according to everyone here, this is paradise and Seattle is the other side of the moon. There are all kinds of wonderful things to do here, like . . . like . . ." She suddenly remembered the poster in the lawyer's window. "Like going to the Forty-eighth Annual Fourth of July Silver Pine Pet Parade."

"What in God's name is a pet parade, Tory? Have you been drinking or something?"

"No, but maybe it would help." She massaged the back of her neck and wondered whether this headache would ever let up. ''This trip hasn't exactly gone according to schedule. The lawyer from San Francisco got sick and couldn't make it to Silver Pine today, but he's coming Tuesday.''

''Tuesday? You mean you won't be back at all until then?''

''Tuesday night, no matter what.''

''Want me to fly down and get you?''

Tory laughed at the thought of Carson in one of his immaculately tailored suits arriving in Silver Pine. Of course, when he piloted his Cessna, he wore something more casual, but whatever he wore, he'd be out of place here. ''No, but thanks for the offer. You have things to do there . . . hors d'oeuvres to test and paintings to hang. Anyway, this isn't really your kind of place.''

''Is there a decent place to stay?''

''Maybe when Annie Oakley was here, but I haven't seen one today. Actually, I'm staying at my new house. I just hope the bats don't get me.''

''That bad?''

''No, not really—but they'd feel right at home here. It's gorgeous, or was at one time before it was engulfed in dust. Three stories, a turret, the works.''

''Sounds like an art gallery to me—everything but the dust, that is.''

''Everything sounds like an art gallery to you. Maybe that's a sign you'd better get back to work on that grand opening of yours. Just a week from tomorrow.''

''Don't remind me. I'm well aware of that terrifying fact, so I'll get back to work now. But what about your place? It sounds spooky. Will you be safe there?''

''Oh, yeah. That's definitely not a problem. I've even acquired a guard dog . . . seems to come with the house.

He belonged to my uncle and keeps wandering back from the neighbor's. And get this. This great big gorgeous house was wide open when I arrived. No one here can even find a key to the place.''

''That's ridiculous.''

''You're telling me? People found it strange that I even asked for a key.''

''Maybe a dog for protection isn't such a bad idea.''

''This dog might damage a burglar if one tripped over him . . . but that's about all he'd do. No, the only things to worry about here are cows, near as I can tell.''

''Cows as in 'moo'?''

''It's a long story. I'll tell you about it sometime.''

''Tory, don't hang up yet. How's your schedule for next week look?''

''Not too good. I'll have a lot of catching up to do when I get back . . . and besides, Carson—''

''I know.'' He cut her off quickly, reluctant to have her tell him again that there was no use hoping. ''Oh, by the way, Gina wanted me to ask if we're up for the club dinner next week. Black tie, of course, and the usual presentation of the Fourth of July race trophies.''

''I guess.'' Her lack of enthusiasm carried across the miles.

''Well, nobody's twisting your arm.''

''We've done the same thing every year for so long.''

''Think of the publicity for Enjouement's opening.''

Tory groaned. ''Yes, I know, and I do want to help you get started, but I'm too tired to think about it right now. It's been a long day and I have a headache.''

''Take a cool shower—they do have running water, don't they?—and order in a nice meal, if you can find one.''

"Order in? You haven't seen Silver Pine. Nothing like Le Chat Sceptique, if that's what you mean—not an escargot or even a latte in sight. Actually, I've been invited to dinner with an elderly neighbor—old friend of my uncle's." Tory didn't volunteer that Brian would be there too.

"And you're going?"

"My choices are strictly limited. And she *can* cook, I'll say that for her."

"How about if I call about nine o'clock to see how you're doing?"

"Oh, Carson—"

"Please, Tory. I'll feel better if I know you got home safely."

"Well, okay, since you put it that way. You're a nice person, Carson. Did I ever mention that? Nine o'clock should be fine. You know that old expression about rolling up the sidewalks at sundown? I think I know where it originated."

By the time Tory figured out the archaic plumbing system in the bathroom off the master bedroom upstairs, her headache was worse and she was ready to forgo any attempt to clean up prior to dinner. However, the heat of the day, coupled with the sight of fluffy white towels and lavender soaps laid out for her by Sarah, convinced her that even if she couldn't grab a quick shower—since there *was* no shower here—for once she could take a bath, assuming she didn't break a leg getting into the gigantic claw-footed tub.

Forty-five minutes later, marvelously refreshed, she emerged from the tepid water, noting as she did so that her headache had completely disappeared. Maybe there was something to be said for taking a leisurely bath rather than her usual quick shower sandwiched between closely scheduled events.

Back in the bedroom, Tory hesitated over the contents of her overnight case, passing up a casual pair of slacks in favor of a long emerald broomstick skirt and matching tunic top. After smoothing the silky fabric over her hips, she accentuated her slender waist with a chunky silver belt. She ran a quick comb through her wavy hair, applied a touch of mascara, and dabbed a hint of Coco Chanel to her throat and wrists to complete her preparations. No need for blusher tonight, she thought, noting the unusually rosy color of her cheeks. She looked accusingly at herself in the full-length antique cheval mirror. *And just who are you dressing up for, my girl?* She didn't bother pretending that she had chosen the outfit merely because it was comfortable, though it was. She knew why she was wearing it. That brief touch of hands earlier . . . well, she just wanted to look her best tonight.

At the raspy buzz of the old-fashioned doorbell, she told her reflection, "I'm just going to dinner, that's all," and watched herself smile. She gave her hair a final pat and, satisfied at last with the results, ran lightly down the broad wooden stairs to open the front door. She looked up, expecting to see Brian's tall form, but he was sitting on the top porch step beside the ever-present Jake, examining Jake's paws one by one. From the back, Tory could see that Brian's dark hair curled damply along the collar of his blue-and-white-striped shirt.

"Aren't you off duty yet?" Tory asked.

"Checking for cheat grass," he answered, getting to his feet and turning to face her. The look on his face told her that he approved of her outfit, but all he said was, "It gets between dogs' toes and burrows in. Causes a lot of trouble if it breaks the skin."

"Find any on Jake?"

"All taken care of. Ready for your guided tour?"

They fell into step and strolled around the side of the house and through the parklike property toward Wolf River some fifty yards away. "These are the ponderosa pines I was telling you about," Brian said, gesturing at some dozen or so trees towering overhead. "Old growth." At her questioning look, he continued, "That means they've never been logged off."

"They're huge," Tory responded.

"And rare nowadays," Brian said. "Some of them along here are four feet in diameter. You don't see too many like this, especially right in a town." He picked up a sprig of pine and held it out to her. "You can tell ponderosa from other pines because it has three needles, see? Lodgepole has just two."

"Ah, now that's a bit of information I've somehow never picked up in downtown Seattle," Tory teased. "Any silver pines around? I assume that's where the town got its name."

"No such critter, I'm afraid. We have ponderosa, also known as yellow pine, and lodgepole, and a few kinds of fir trees, but no silver pine. I think maybe somebody was out walking in the moonlight one time and got a little poetic, but you be sure and let me know if you see any."

Tory laughed. "I'll do that. Whether these are silver pines or not, they're beautiful—and the needles feel wonderful underfoot, all soft and springy."

"They are that, I'll grant you, but let's see how you feel about walking along here in a couple of minutes,"

Brian answered, glancing at the green velvet ballet slippers on her feet. "Your shoes aren't exactly designed for this terrain."

"When I'm invited next door for dinner in Seattle, I don't usually have to wear hiking boots," Tory said.

"You're not in Seattle," Brian said. As the sound of the swiftly flowing river grew louder, he raised his voice and gestured to the right. There, a small irrigation ditch entered the river at a right angle to the riverbank, interrupting the trail. Brian took Tory's hand and assisted her as she jumped gracefully from one side to the other.

"That wasn't so bad," she said.

"That wasn't the worst of it. Look." Brian pointed to a spongy area ahead. "The ground is saturated along here. You'll ruin those shoes."

"Why didn't you tell me that before we left?"

Without answering, he swept her effortlessly into his arms and carried her across the uneven ground for several minutes without speaking. Surprised at first, Tory breathed in Brian's clean, soap smell and found that she didn't want to break the silence either. When he set her down at last on the dry lawn that framed Sarah's house, Tory felt strangely light-headed, almost as though she were emerging from a dream.

Sarah burst out the back door, letting the wooden screen slap closed behind her. "There you are . . . and don't you look nice? Doesn't she look nice, Brian?" Glancing at her nephew with surprise, she continued, "You look nice, too, Brian. Been a long time since I've seen you in anything but jeans. Well, don't just stand there. Come on in. Supper's about ready, such as it is. Potluck, of course."

Up the steps, through a screened back porch and

kitchen piled high with pots and pans, Sarah hurried
them along, saying "Don't look, don't look" all the
while until she ushered them into the cool, high-
ceilinged dining room. The table was set with a delicate
white lace cloth and bone china in an old fashioned pattern bordered with flowers. Did people really still sit
down to eat like this at home? Tory had seen such settings only in expensive Victorian restaurants. She pic-
tured her usual meals at the penthouse, meals she
frequently consumed while standing by the counter, cra-
dling a phone between her ear and shoulder while holding a fork in one hand and a little white box of take-out
food in the other.

"Brian, could you bring in the soup?" Sarah asked.
"No, never mind. You pull out Tory's chair and I'll get
the soup."

With a slight smile and a bow, Brian held Tory's chair
for her and then seated himself opposite. Sarah brought
in a flowered tureen that matched the china on the table.
"Hope you like cucumber soup. On such a hot night, it
sounded good to me," she said as she ladled it out.

Before Tory could so much as taste the chilled cucumber soup, Sarah burst out happily, "I'm so glad you
changed your mind about staying the night, dear. Does
that mean you might be staying even longer?"

Tory put down the heavy silver soup spoon. "Not
much longer . . . several days at most."

"But that's wonderful. That means you'll be here all
weekend."

"Till Tuesday."

"Oh, good. You'll be here for the parade then. It's
lots of fun . . . and by then maybe we'll have convinced
you that Virgil Wright and Arlie Lind don't speak for

the whole town. And no matter what Harriet Corcoran's la-di-da plans are for . . ." She trailed off, looking stricken. "Brian, why didn't you stop me?" She turned to Tory and explained, "Brian and I made a pact not to bother you tonight about your plans. I was so cross with him for the way he treated you earlier. Well, not one word about plans tonight. Right, Brian? You're not to say a word." She patted Tory's hand and whispered, "But the very idea of a big old ugly office building alongside the river . . . well . . . and besides, it would be such fun to have you as a neighbor."

Not likely, Tory thought, but she made no comment as she dipped her spoon into the soup. Its icy tartness and the delicate hint of dill made her wonder why she'd always dismissed cucumber soup as bland. As the conversation turned to general topics, Tory relaxed and found herself enjoying the meal enormously. She noted with some amusement that Sarah's idea of a simple potluck dinner included fresh tomatoes and green beans from her garden, homemade biscuits, fried chicken, and iced tea. Just when Tory thought she could eat no more, Sarah produced a steaming blackberry cobbler topped with homemade vanilla ice cream.

As they relaxed over their after-dinner coffee, Tory noticed an elegant arrangement of roses in various shades of red and pink in a crystal vase on the sideboard. "How gorgeous . . . the flowers and the vase. They're perfect together."

"Your aunt gave me that vase one Christmas. Said she admired my roses and thought this would set them off. She was right too. Of course her roses were something special too . . . you've probably noticed." She sighed. "It's been two years since she died, and I still miss her. Your uncle never quite got over losing her, you know. All those silly love stories on television don't hold a candle to their relationship, and that's a fact. Speaking of television, *Red River* is on tonight and I've been wanting to see it.''

''Again?'' asked Brian.

''Yes, again. Don't you get smart with me, young man. Maybe you two wouldn't mind if I excuse myself now? John Wayne, you know,'' she added by way of explanation.

''Might as well get ready to leave, Tory. I never could compete with the Duke,'' Brian said, rising. ''Great meal, as usual, Aunt Sarah. Thanks for agreeing to come, Tory, so she'd at least feed me before kicking me out.''

''Why, Brian Rafferty. You know very well I'll be glad to feed you anytime you want. You need some fattening up, I'm bound to say—Monica never did understand that.'' She turned to Tory. ''The less said about that one, the better.''

''We'd better be going, Aunt Sarah. You'll miss your movie.''

''He means I'm talking too much. All right, Brian. I know, I know.''

''Can't we help with the dishes first?'' Tory asked.

''Heavens, no. Won't take but a minute. You two go along now,'' she said as she swept them out the door.

Jake was waiting outside. ''Looks like you've got yourself a dog.'' Brian said.

''He does seem pretty friendly.''

''Yeah, he's a good old dog. We can go back along the road if you'd prefer.''

''That stretch along the river is so beautiful though

... let's go that way.'' Tory shivered as she remembered the feel of his arms around her.

''You're cold?''

''No.''

''Here, take my jacket.'' Brian wrapped her in his tan windbreaker, so large that she almost disappeared inside. She held up her arms to show the sleeves trailing some inches below her hands.

They turned companionably and started across the lawn, Jake falling into place behind them. The night sounds of crickets surrounded them in the near darkness. This time when they reached the spongy ground and Brian moved to pick her up, she was ready for it, but his nearness made no less impact on her than before. She wound her arms around his neck to hold on, though she knew there was no need. She'd never in her life felt safer than at that moment.

All too soon they reached dry ground, and he slowly put her down. When they came to the irrigation ditch, once again he held her hand as she jumped the small barrier. They didn't speak as they retraced their earlier steps over the soft pine needles. Presently, her uncle's house appeared ahead, its solid bulk visible through the trees. The one light she'd left burning cast a soft glow over the porch. The light scent of the honeysuckle by the door added to the spell of the summer evening. They stood for a long moment facing each other at the foot of the steps. Tory felt the blood thundering in her ears.

Inside the house, the phone began to ring. Nuts, she thought. Carson calling to make sure she was safely home. He was a nice guy and a concerned friend, but he had a lousy sense of timing.

She asked, "Would you like to come in? I have some apple cake left."

"I'd better go," Brian answered. "You'll be all right?"

"With Jake on guard here? Of course, I'll be fine." The ringing continued.

"Well, you'd better answer that phone. Somebody sounds persistent. Good night."

"Good night, Brian . . . and . . . thanks for the deluxe tour."

"Anytime."

Chapter Three

Warm rays of sunlight playing over her face awakened Tory. She rolled over to check her digital travel alarm, and then did a double take at the numbers being displayed—8:17. Was that possible? She was always up by 4:30 to allow herself time for a workout at the Pacific Club and a quick peek at *The Wall Street Journal* before battling the crosstown Seattle traffic in order to reach Northwest Financial Management headquarters by 6:30. Since her father's death, she had become the first broker to show up each morning; when he had been alive, he often arrived before daybreak.

In fact, she had established the habit of going in before regular business hours as a way of spending time with him. This early morning time had provided her with her best chance to catch him between business trips. He'd stop by her door now and then for a brief comment, and once in a great while he'd come in to perch on one

38

corner of her desk for a precious five minutes. Of course, the talk always centered around work. She had learned that conversation about pending stock mergers and the rise and fall of the market caught his interest more than anything else she could possibly say, so she deliberately confined her comments to those subjects. Eventually, he'd started asking her advice on trades and including her in working lunches with select clients.

It wasn't until much later that Tory had realized how isolated her quiet mother must have felt when her husband and daughter followed their lengthy days at work together with endless hours of discussion on the same topics at home. Though her mother had willingly provided the seed money from her own family holdings to establish NFM, she had never shared her husband's interest in the financial world. She had wanted only to help her handsome, driven husband succeed in his chosen profession, and she had certainly done that. When her daughter followed so eagerly in her father's footsteps, what had her mother thought of it? Tory had never bothered to ask. Her mother was always just . . . there . . . in the background, smiling, smoothing the path of her busy family, leaving Tory and her father free to devote their time and energy to the ever more successful cause of building NFM.

Those clients who had at first dismissed Tory as the boss's ornamental but exceedingly young daughter had soon come to see her as a power in her own right at NFM. Thus, when a plane crash a year ago took the lives of both her parents as they journeyed to Zurich for an international stock symposium, her determined return to work a week after the funeral, combined with her well-crafted financial advice, convinced a number of her father's best clients to stay on with her. They had found no reason to regret their decision since. Tory's fourteen-hour days and sound financial instincts had paid off handsomely for them all.

That pressure-packed environment seemed far, far away from the lazy sunlit morning that stretched ahead of her in Silver Pine. Today, for a change, Tory faced no deadlines, though of course she had brought along her laptop computer and a heavy briefcase.

She threw aside the well-worn quilt and swung her slender legs over the side of the high, mahogany bed, wondering how someone had maneuvered this imposing piece of furniture up the stairs and into the bedroom. The towering headboard alone surely weighed several hundred pounds. At the end of the bed stood a tufted leather fainting couch with rounded legs, and across the room a bentwood rocking chair was angled toward the little fireplace on that wall. Why lug this heavy furniture all the way up to the second floor? Surely there was some other room downstairs that would be suitable as the master bedroom, but she had been so tired last night that she hadn't even looked through the entire house. Well, maybe later. Besides, she could guess at one reason for choosing this large, sunny room as a place to spend a lot of time.

The turret that Tory had noticed yesterday opened off this room, letting in the welcome morning light and providing extra space and an extraordinary view. A padded brocade window seat provided an invitation to sit and look out at the trees and the river beyond them. A heavy white afghan and some tasseled scarlet pillows rested casually on the window seat, almost as though someone had thrown them there only a few moments before and would be returning soon. Tory could imagine a young woman expressing to her husband the wish to make this charming room their own, and she could see with equal clarity an earnest young husband doing whatever was necessary to make this room the sanctuary his beloved wife wanted. Tory watched the intermittent lift of the lacy curtains as a breeze worked gently at the custom-designed open turret windows. How peaceful this room was, how perfectly . . . useless. .

She shook her head at her inactivity. Though her father had talked only rarely about Silver Pine, she did remember him saying more than once, as though baffled at such an attitude, "Nothing much ever gets done there, and nobody even seems to care." She could see why that might be true, if everyone reacted to the atmosphere the way she seemed to be doing this morning. Whatever the reason, she certainly wasn't accomplishing anything by sitting here watching the curtains blow in the breeze.

For someone who liked quick, efficient showers, Tory found this bathroom something of a change. Her aunt and uncle had apparently lived their lives at a more lei-surely pace than Tory usually did. She eyed the high, claw-footed tub as an enemy of the efficient use of her time, then reminded herself that she wasn't required to sit back and soak for forty-five minutes as she had last night. Turning the old-fashioned brass taps, she released an abundance of hot water into the tub, to which she added bath salts from a delicate glass jar standing nearby. The aroma of lavender filled the room. Not bad, she thought, as she shrugged out of her lacy nightgown and hung it on a heavy brass rod behind the door. She stepped into the tub, thinking that she could take a five-minute bath as easily as a five-minute shower.

Forty-five relaxed, luxurious minutes later, she padded downstairs wearing huaraches, a peach-colored tank top, and white cotton shorts. She resisted the urge to explore the house, thinking that she'd wasted enough time already this morning by again succumbing to the peacefulness of the warm bath, and now she really would have to get to work.

The glossy surface of the enormous dining room table seemed to be an excellent place to set up her office. An inspection of the massive mahogany cupboards and drawers that ringed the dining room unearthed an impressive array of silver and china, enough crystal to outfit a restaurant, and, at last, a padded cover to protect the table. Judging from the number of place settings she found, she concluded that her aunt and uncle must have done a lot of entertaining in their home. Her own parents rarely invited anyone to dine with them at home, but instead preferred to do whatever business entertaining was necessary at one of the upscale Seattle restaurants. As for entertaining people on a strictly social basis, having nothing to do with business contacts, she really couldn't remember any such gatherings. Somehow, from the little she had gathered about her aunt and uncle, she suspected that their home had been filled with friends, not business associates.

Tory extended the modem cord out to the front hall and plugged it into the one telephone jack in the house. Then she booted up her computer and resolutely plunged back into the familiar world of business. Soon she was completely engrossed in the stock market report, noting with satisfaction that the newly announced Bethway–National Data merger had caused a three-point surge in the stock she had been recommending for weeks.

She paused once to venture as far as the huge, inefficient kitchen in search of a cup of coffee. A half-empty jar of Nescafé was the only coffee to be found in the high white cupboards. Murmuring ''beggars can't be choosers,'' she heated some water in a granite coffeepot on the fifties-era Hotpoint electric stove. Next to it stood an ancient wood stove with SEARS & ROEBUCK emblazoned across its ornate black oven door. A kitchen big enough for two stoves? Her kitchen in Seattle barely had room for her microwave, and that was about all she ever used anyway. This one not only had two stoves, but plenty of room for the refrigerator and a kitchen table and four chairs as well. A faded rag rug covered the space under the table, bundles of herbs hung from a line strung along the far wall, and a complete set of tan mixing bowls with a thick blue stripe claimed the space over the sink. The rest of the house might have been filled with elegant furnishings, but this room had been left as a cozy, ordinary work space.

She grimaced at the bitter taste of the Nescafé and cut another piece of the still-delicious apple cake. Well, the coffee was hot anyway, and the buttery cake made up for a lot. Carrying the cake and the coffee, she returned to the familiar blinking cursor on her computer screen. Several hours later, she was still hard at work, but the temperature in the dining room had risen, even with all the windows thrown wide open. She wasn't used to working in a room without air-conditioning, and her tank top was damp and clinging to her back.

Brushing back moist tendrils of hair that curled around her face, Tory returned to the kitchen in search of Sarah's lemonade. The Frigidaire refrigerator looked about the same age as the electric stove, and the icy buildup around the tiny freezing compartment nestled in the middle of the refrigerated section showed that it was manufactured before anyone had perfected a frost-free unit. Still, the ice cube trays were full, and she wrestled one of them out of its frosty bed and ran it under the faucet until the cubes came loose. Bless you, Sarah, she thought as she dropped a few pieces into a tall glass. The icy liquid tasted even better than it had yesterday. Must be the mint. Sarah was right. Refilling the glass to the top, she took it with her and returned to the neat piles of paper spread on the table.

Her neck was stiff by the time a distant rhythmic sound from outside penetrated her consciousness. Grateful for an excuse to stand up, she slipped her feet into the huaraches and opened the front door. Experienced now, she didn't trip over Jake lying as usual across the threshold, but stepped over him casually and descended the porch steps. She waited at the bottom of the steps until he got to his feet and fell into place behind her. Together, they retraced the route through the parklike setting between the house and river and then turned to follow the riverbank toward Sarah's house. The sound grew louder as they approached Sarah's property.

Brian, shirt off and torso gleaming with sweat, methodically chopped at a log in the side yard, a mound of cut wood already piled neatly beside him. From the size of the stack, he must have been at it for some time.

Tory tried to imagine Carson chopping wood, but the picture just wouldn't come. Carson couldn't even eat a hamburger in the car without having to stop and wash. He hated getting his hands dirty. Maybe that explained the small roll of fat starting to appear above his waistband, in spite of his haphazard attempts to exercise.

Brian apparently had no such problems—either with getting his hands dirty or staying in shape.

"Hello there," she called. "Isn't it a little hot to be swinging an ax?"

"Far as I'm concerned, it is." Brian lowered the ax and mopped his brow. "But have you ever tried telling Sarah something she didn't want to hear?"

Tory laughed. "Well, I guess you do owe her for that wonderful dinner, but then so do I. Should I offer to hoe the garden?"

"Over Sarah's dead body. Nobody touches her garden but her."

"Dishes?"

"Done."

"What do you suggest?"

"How about getting me a drink of water?"

"I can do better than that. Do you think she'll let you stop long enough for a glass of lemonade? She made it, so she ought to approve."

Sarah emerged from the house just then. "You make me sound like some kind of slave driver. Of course you can have some lemonade, Brian. In fact, I've made a little lunch that would work just fine for a picnic. Why don't you show Tory around the area?"

"I thought you called me because you wanted this wood chopped?"

"It's July, Brian. Why would I need it done now?"

"But you said—"

"Well then, it's all settled. I'll get the basket."

Brian turned with a grin to Tory. "Have I just been fired?"

"Sounds like it."

"Help me make my getaway before she changes her mind."

Tory started to shake her head as she remembered the unfinished work piled on the dining room table. She considered all the telephone calls and e-mail messages she should return . . . and then she looked at Brian. "I'll get the lemonade."

As Tory ran lightly across the grass toward the house, Jake suddenly detoured toward one of the giant old pine trees, his tail waving a greeting. The sound of smothered giggles greeted his arrival, and his tail spiraled even more frantically in response. Curious, Tory circled the tree until she found the source of the giggles. Two young girls, one short and the other tall, stood plastered against the back side of the tree. Jake danced back and forth between them and Tory.

"Hi," Tory ventured.

The giggles subsided and the two answered in unison, "Hi." The taller of the two stepped out a pace and said, "You're going to live in Jim's house. That means we'll be neighbors. Jim said we could play here."

"Well—" Tory began.

"It's a neat place to play. And he always let Jake come for walks with us."

Tory tried again. "Well—"

"So we were wondering, me and Amy, if that's still okay with you. This is Amy. She lives on the other side of me"—she waved an arm casually back over her shoulder—"but she likes Jake too, and Jim said we could walk Jake in the pet parade this year. Course that was before . . ." She trailed off, uncertain. "Oh, I'm supposed to say I'm sorry about Jim . . . he was your uncle, right? He was really nice and . . . and we're sorry he died.'' She shifted uncomfortably from one leg to the other as if trying to decide whether she had covered the topic sufficiently. Apparently satisfied, she continued with the topic she really wanted to cover. ''See, the way it works, you get to decorate your dog . . . or whatever pet you bring—''

''Yes, I know how it works,'' Tory said. The pet parade again. It seemed to crop up in every Silver Pine conversation and obviously was the high point of the week here for a lot of people. From the way Jake was jumping around, he'd be all for it too. ''Okay, I guess, if you have a leash—''

''Oh, Jim had one, or maybe Sarah has it now . . . but we'll take real good care of Jake and bring him right back after—''

''Getting him back here doesn't seem to be much of a problem,'' Tory said dryly.

''Then we can do it? It's okay with you?''

''Sure. That'll be fine.'' In reaction to her words, both girls immediately joined Jake in jumping around. Tory didn't remember any announcement of hers at NFM ever being greeted with anything like the enthusiasm this one seemed to produce.

''You won't be sorry. He'll be the best dog in the parade this year, just wait.''

''I'm sure he will.''

''You're coming to see the parade, aren't you?''

''I hadn't planned to . . . I've got lots to do . . . and it's really more for kids, isn't it?''

''Oh, no,'' Amy piped up at last, carried away with the success of their petition. ''Everybody goes. We can't have pets at our house because my brother is allergic, but Mom and Dad and Todd—that's my brother—go anyway. There are goats and chickens . . . and horses, and even a goldfish last year.''

''A goldfish?''

''Course, he was in a fishbowl . . . in a wagon . . . but one year—''

Apparently, once Amy got started, she was good for a couple of hours. In the interest of speed, Tory broke in. ''Okay, okay. I'll come. The goldfish decided it.''

''But you'll look specially for Jake, won't you?''

''Specially.''

''You know, there may not be a goldfish this year.''

''That's okay. I'll come anyway.''

''We'll be over early to get Jake.''

''Not too early. What time's the parade?''

Two stricken looks. Obviously, they didn't portion out their time as carefully as those in the adult world. ''Check with your mothers, okay? Just don't make it before nine o'clock. Jake will be here whenever you arrive.''

''And it's okay if we play here . . . like before?''

''Sure, why not?'' A beautiful day, a picnic with a handsome man . . . things in Silver Pine were looking up.

Chapter Four

Brian reached for the wicker basket Sarah held out. "I've got to tell her," he said. "If it felt awkward to avoid the subject of NorthPointe last night, it's going to feel even more ridiculous to dodge it today."

Sarah shook her head and grabbed back the basket in alarm. "Brian Rafferty, you're six kinds of a fool! Remember Tory's first impression of Silver Pine, thanks to you?"

"But the longer I go—"

"Just give it a little more time. Let her get comfortable, see what a nice place this is, and then she'll be a lot more likely to listen to what you have to say Monday. Look how nice our evening was last night . . . you found plenty to say without bringing that up, didn't you? And now this picnic today—don't ruin everything by trying to sell her on your proposal."

"I'm not meaning to sell her on anything today . . .

but it just seems . . . well, underhanded. I ought to say something, sort of lay things out plain before—''

''Before what? Before she starts thinking that Silver Pine's a nice place just the way it is? Before she starts thinking that you're . . . well, attractive? Don't give me that look. Even if I can remember a whole lot of block-headed stunts you pulled as a kid, I can still see that you've grown into a man some women might call attractive. Keeping quiet isn't underhanded. It's just . . . well, it's strategy, that's what it is . . . putting your best foot forward, Brian. You two were getting along last night . . . right?''

''Pretty well,'' he agreed. Though he tried to sound noncommittal, Brian knew that his words didn't begin to cover his reaction to Tory last night—the way she fit so easily into his arms, her throaty laugh, the clean smell of her hair.

''You don't fool me a bit, Brian. That girl's a knock-out, and if you can't see that, then you're dull as dirt and not worth my time. You want her to go back to looking at you the way she did yesterday afternoon— sort of like a snake she'd like to stomp?''

Brian laughed. ''Let's get our projects straight. Are you trying to keep Tory from selling her property to California Development or angling to find me a wife?''

''Ever heard of having your cake and eating it too?'' Sarah tried to look sly, but her open, friendly face betrayed her. ''Of course I want to slow down those skunks, but I also want to see you happy. Oh, Brian, Tory's everything you'd ever want—nothing like that Monica.'' She couldn't even say the name without pursing her lips in disapproval.

''Don't start,'' Brian warned her.

"I know, water under the bridge," she answered, "but I had her pegged right from the start."

"Here we go," Brian said, nodding. This was an old story. "Why, I remember at dinner—"

"Don't you sass me, young man, but—now that you mention it—the way that Monica turned up her nose, complaining my cooking was too rich . . . You better listen to me this time. Tory liked my cucumber soup."

"Well, that's certainly the clincher, isn't it?"

"I was right about that Monica."

"Yes, but—"

"But nothing. C'mon, Brian. Don't spoil today by blurting out that you're one of those council members bent on changing her mind about selling. Just enjoy your picnic. Talk about whatever young people talk about on picnics these days, and then, by tomorrow, you can sort of ease her into the whole idea. After all, you and Stu won't be meeting her officially until Monday, so there's lots of time over the weekend for you to get around to talking with her about your ideas for Silver Pine."

"I really don't think this is a good idea, Sarah."

"You have something against giving that poor girl just one more peaceful day without people yammering at her about sell this or do that? Last night was such fun when we didn't bring it up. You'll at least admit that, won't you?"

"Well, yes," Brian acknowledged. It was true that Tory had seemed right at home, laughing and matching them story for story at the dinner table. No one had missed the controversial topic even one little bit.

"See? That's it then," she said triumphantly. "For your poor old aunt?"

"For my scheming old aunt. Well, just for today. To-morrow, I'm telling her—with no arguments from you."

"You promise now?"

"Promise."

"Fair enough. Now here's your picnic lunch." She relinquished the basket at last.

"Thank you, ma'am. Any more instructions? Want to check that I washed behind my ears?"

"Now you're being silly. Get out of here. Why are you standing here talking to me when you have a beautiful woman next door just dying to have you take her on a tour of the local sights?"

Brian gave her a peck on the cheek. "Aunt Sarah, you're amazing. Okay, I'm going, I'm going, but I still think—"

"Don't think. Just have a good time. Tomorrow you can go back to saving this place from California Development. NorthPointe, my foot!"

Brian's misgivings melted under the blaze of Tory's smile as he pulled up in front of her house. The boyish white baseball cap she wore in no way hid her beauty. Was there a chance such a woman might look twice at him? She'd seemed interested last night, all friendly and agreeable, but maybe he was mistaking politeness for something more. After all, she and Monica came from the same world of country club connections and high finance. They were used to charming people . . . absorbing the proper technique along with their ballet classes and table manners. Monica had been charming all right, up until the moment someone didn't fall into line with her plans. That was when her veneer of softness cracked. She had certainly fooled him, long enough to get an engagement ring on her finger, at least. Was it possible that Tory was just as phony?

But he had to look at his own actions, too. How honest was he being with Tory in failing to tell her right away about his opposition to California Development and all they stood for? Maybe he should go back and get Sarah to release him from his promise.

Still, possibly Sarah was right. Tory had just met him. What credibility did he have at this point to say, ''Hi, I'm Brian, and you're a fool for selling to those sharks''? She was a businesswoman, and unless he could make her understand the unscrupulousness of this particular developer, he would be wasting his breath. After all, hadn't he been talking himself hoarse recently trying to get some people he'd known for years—even others on the Silver Pine City Council—to listen to him? Arlie and Virgil welcomed the changes, and the money, that California Development's NorthPointe project was bringing to the area. The dangers they brought were less apparent, but Brian had seen them in action before, and he knew how skillful they were at concealing their true agenda until they had control of a situation.

Tory pulled open the passenger-side door and gave him an impish grin. ''What a glorious day for a drive. I feel that I'm twelve years old and playing hookey— which I never actually did, I might mention. But this picnic sure beats looking at a spreadsheet today.''

''I'm not much for spreadsheets at any time, but I did become quite an expert on playing hookey when I was about twelve,'' Brian said. The prospect of spending the afternoon driving around the area with this smiling, relaxed young woman was much more inviting than conducting serious discussions about real estate and community planning. Maybe Sarah was right. One day's delay couldn't make all that much difference. "Just let me clear a few things off the seat and we'll go."

"A few things?"

Brian stuffed a clipboard and three worn copies of the *Journal of the American Veterinary Medical Association* behind the seat. "This truck does double duty as an office," he explained, tossing a pair of muddy rubber boots and a medical kit into the bed of the pickup.

Tory held up a metal contraption resembling a bridle from the floor on her side of the cab.

"Twitch handle," Brian said, "for horses. Keeps me from getting bitten when things get rough."

"Fun job," Tory said. She offered him a squashed bag of Fritos and several empty Squirt cans. "Is your truck a restaurant too?"

"The finest—well, not quite as fine as Sarah's place, of course. Here, give me that stuff." He rounded the truck and added her collection to the other items in back. Taking the jug of lemonade from her as well, he set it carefully in a cardboard box next to the picnic hamper, which he then pulled open to show her what Sarah had packed. "No room here for so much as another slice of salami," he said. "Hope you're hungry."

Tory looked over the side at the wicker basket, full to the top, and spoke with wonder. "She just happened to have all this food on hand?"

"Can't say for sure. She's always cooking something, of course, but she's taken a special liking to you. . . ." Tory was standing close to him, her head tilted far back as she looked up into his face. Brian lost track of what he had been about to say. She had the clearest green eyes he'd ever seen.

"And?"

"And . . . ah . . . I think she just wanted to be friendly." He finally brought his thoughts under control. "Lucky for me that I happened to be around at the right time. When I'm not eating in the truck, I take in a lot of meals standing up by the counter."

"Me too," Tory said. "Sarah's cooking may ruin me forever for that."

"Well, as long as she went to all this trouble," Brian said with mock seriousness, "I think we're duty bound to eat our way through this lunch—even if it takes the rest of the day."

"What a wonderful prospect."

"So you don't mind if we're out all afternoon? You seemed to have some work to do . . . ?" He paused, letting the question hang in the air.

"Oh, that," Tory responded. Her smile faded. "Well, yes, I do have some. Quite a lot of it, in fact."

Brian waited while she considered. He wanted to kick himself for even mentioning work and bringing yesterday's tense look back to her face, even momentarily. "Sarah says you need a day's vacation in the high desert fresh air more than you need . . . anything more serious. That's probably why she made this picnic."

Apparently, Tory had reached the same conclusion. She smiled again, her decision made. "Work can wait. I haven't taken a day off in a long while, and we certainly wouldn't want to be rude to Sarah, so if it takes all day, it takes all day."

"You got it." Brian said with relief. "What do you think . . . ?" he asked, motioning to Jake standing hopefully nearby. He might as well find out right away how she felt about having dogs around. Monica thought all animals belonged in zoos.

"You know, it's sort of funny. I've always been afraid of dogs, maybe because I've never had one of my own, but Jake's good company. Sure, let him come."

"Great!" This day was looking better and better. "What's a ride in the country without a dog? Besides, I'll bet he'd be willing to help us with this mountain of food."

"Either he helps, or we'd better find a lost and hungry party of hikers somewhere along the way."

The two-lane highway with the distinctive red cinder roadbed typical of central Oregon unwound before them as they drove southwest toward snowcapped mountains that glistened in the sun. The road climbed steadily out of the high desert that surrounded Silver Pine, and soon the juniper and sagebrush along the route gave way on both sides to pine trees interrupted by occasional rock outcroppings. Brian pointed out geologic formations as they drove, while Tory listened and asked intelligent questions that indicated both her lively mind and her lack of experience in the back country. An occasional mule deer bounded across the road, startling her and causing Jake to whine with excitement.

"You'd just love to chase one of those guys, wouldn't you, Jake?" Brian threw an arm over him and ruffled his soft fur. "If you're not real familiar with dogs, Tory, I should tell you that golden retrievers are about the best-tempered dogs around."

"I believe you. Jake wasn't guarding the house too effectively the other day."

"No, but he'd be great for making a place seem less lonely." Now why did I say a dumb thing like that? he thought. Someone like Tory wouldn't ever have to worry about being lonely. He blundered on, "I mean, not that you'd ever—"

Tory rescued him. "I know what you mean. He's so happy all the time. It's bound to make the people around him feel cheerful."

"Your uncle sure loved him. That dog provided a lot of company for Jim after Ellen died . . . and from the way Jake keeps turning up at the house, I'd guess Jake misses him, too. They helped each other. Jake needed a home and Jim needed a friend. Not that Jim didn't have a bushel of friends around here, but he and Ellen were so close . . . well, they had about the happiest marriage I ever saw. You didn't know them at all?"

"My family didn't talk about Silver Pine. Father just didn't seem interested in it, and Mother always followed his lead in things like that . . . pretty much everything else too. I never thought about it before, but now it does seem sort of strange."

Brian could tell that what was common knowledge in Silver Pine about Tory's father obviously wasn't part of what she knew—and he wasn't going to make it his business to tell her. After all, what woman wanted to hear that her father had been generally considered stuck up, someone who used to give the impression, even as a kid, that he was much too good for his own hometown? And even if Brian had thought Tory should know what people thought about her father, he wouldn't want to be the one to say anything to make her feel sad. When she smiled, she lit up everything around her, and when she smiled especially at him, he wanted to pop a wheelie on his bike or skip rocks on a lake like a moonstruck ten-year-old—anything to make her look at him like that again. If only he could get rid of the nagging feeling that he'd made a mistake in promising Sarah—

"What's that peak?" Tory asked, breaking into his thoughts.

"One of the Beacons," he answered. "There's a couple more farther north. See how they all line up?"

"I see them, but aren't beacons usually associated with the coast?"

"Maybe somebody was really lost . . . thought they were getting close to the Pacific Ocean instead of smack in the middle of the Cascade Mountains. Just ahead is Searchlight Butte, part of the same formation. Used to be called Searchlight Butte anyway. Not anymore though. Not fancy enough for the California Development people. They're the ones developing NorthPointe, and they managed to get the Oregon Geographic Names Board to rename the poor old butte Lodestar Peak. Guess it goes better with their whole compass image: North-Pointe here, SouthPointe in California. For all I know, they'll put NorthwestPointe somewhere up near Portland, and who knows what else they'll think up? Lots of directions left to use. All with those silly *e*'s stuck on the end of each name." *Careful, Brian,* he thought. *Your attitude's showing.*

"So that'll be the new ski resort?" Tory asked. "You don't sound very impressed."

"That's it, and I'm not. Look at the hillside, all broken up with gashes and slashes. And that's just the start of their plans."

"I'll admit it looks pretty bad right now, but give them the benefit of the doubt. Of course things are a mess when they're right in the midst of building. Maybe you don't like skiing . . . or are you just opposed to progress on general principal?''

"Depends on how you define progress. Change'll come, one way or another, but some companies are worse than others—and, frankly, this one stinks.''

"Why's that? No, go ahead. I'd like to hear what you think, because I talked to some of the people involved with this project and they seemed to be right on top of things, very professional. You know that they plan to make some Silver Pine area residents very rich.''

"Oh, I'm sure that they do.''

"And that's bad?''

"Not necessarily. Don't get me wrong—I like making money as well as the next guy, and I do like to ski, by the way—but look . . . have you ever heard of the High Desert Land Trust?''

"I hadn't before yesterday when Don Thorne mentioned it. He said my uncle worked with them and had left them a sizable amount of money in his will.''

"That's right. He was deeply committed to their idea of buying up land and holding it in trust for the good of the community.''

"Holding it as in 'failing to develop it'?'' She shook her head. "No wonder he and my father didn't spend much time together. Father would turn over in his grave at the thought of wasting the potential of moneymaking property for some ill-defined purpose like that. In fact, I'm surprised my uncle found a way to save enough money to allow him to bequeath them anything if that was a sample of the business decisions he made. Very noble, but hardly profitable.''

He bit back his first response and looked at her thoughtfully. This conversation was veering too close to the forbidden topic, and Brian was uncomfortably aware of how much Tory's attitudes about the importance and use of money had been influenced by her father. He could also see why the old-timers around town said that Jim and his brother Richard were as different as night and day. "I keep forgetting you didn't know Jim. He'd laugh if you called him noble, though I guess he'd qualify in a quiet way. I'd call him far-seeing and effective, taking the long view to protect the quality of life he valued in this community. I'll tell you this . . . he was a good man."

"You knew him well?"

"Sure. Hard not to in a place like this. And besides, we worked together on . . . on this and that around town. Great guy, Jim, always helping out other people. By the way, the land trust will be using his money to try to buy up some of this land along here between town and Searchlight Butte—oh, I keep forgetting: Lodestar Peak—to form sort of a buffer zone around Silver Pine."

"But it's a long way from the ski country down into town. Don't those thirty or whatever miles in between form a buffer zone all by themselves? Aren't there ranches and farms in between?"

"More like forty miles, but those guys have sort of a 'camel's nose under the edge of the tent' approach to this area. You know the old saying—if you let a camel get his nose inside the tent, at first it seems like no big deal, but you'd better think again because soon enough you'll have the whole darn critter inside with you."

"And?"

"And I know some ranchers between town and the resort area wouldn't be against turning a fast buck, if the chance came along."

"And?"

"And—bottom line—I'd rather look at ranch land and pine trees than share the countryside with these four-lane NorthPointe guys. They're fast talkers and, believe me, they're not planning to confine their operations to property way out in the middle of nowhere."

"The proverbial city slickers?"

"They'd certainly qualify. Yeah, you could call them that."

"I don't mean to be disagreeable, but you sound awfully suspicious. Do you think they sit around twirling their black mustaches or something? They're reputable businessmen, not riverboat gamblers, and they've been doing business a long time. When I talked to them about buying my property, they specifically assured me they have no intention of moving in the direction of town."

"Want to buy a bridge, lady? If you believe what they said, I'd like to sell you one. Tell me this: Why do you suppose they want your property, if it's so far from their resort?"

"They explained that. It's just a matter of convenience to have an office in town instead of out in the middle of the mountains."

"Translation: They want to keep things quiet while they buy up property. That's the way they work. Watch them swing into action once they've got what they want all lined up. I'm sure they made everything sound wonderful. They talk a great game."

"Give me one solid complaint about them."

"How much time have you got?"

"Oh, come on. Is it possible you don't have a specific objection? In my business, I come across a lot of people who just don't like change. Usually their objections disappear when they see how much money a certain kind of change can bring to their lives.''

Brian gave her a long look before answering. Maybe it was a good thing he hadn't tried to talk specifically about his opposition to California Development before this. She still hadn't quite grasped the essence of what he valued about the quality of life in Silver Pine. She'd been isolated in her sterile, high-priced world for a long time, a world in which making money was of paramount importance. He wished she'd spent her childhood absorbing the attitudes of her uncle instead of her father. ''Well, now that you mention it, I personally wouldn't mind at all if Silver Pine stayed exactly the way it is, but that's not realistic. Seems to me the trick is to help it grow in a way that will keep the best parts of it through the inevitable changes to come. You want a specific example of why I don't like California Development and their NorthPointe project? I'll give you one. What would you say about a company riding roughshod over local zoning regulations by putting blue plastic tape around all the trees they planned to cut down?''

''What's wrong with that?''

''Nothing, if they left it at that, or waited until they had proper authorization to go ahead. But their trick was to cut the trees down before anyone had a chance to say they couldn't, in cases where they couldn't manipulate the zoning laws, that is. Later, they claimed they'd made a mistake.''

''They'd be fined for doing something like that.''

''So what? They could afford to pay a hefty fine, and by then the trees were gone. Oh, what a shame. That's the kind of stunt I mean.''

''And you've seen this situation yourself?''

"Yes. Different state, same company."

"Maybe they did make a mistake. That can happen, you know."

Change the subject. Dangerous ground here, Brian thought. The more he talked about the corrupt business practices of California Development, the more his anger rose. Still, a promise was a promise. With some effort, he forced his voice to a more neutral tone and his attention to a less upsetting topic. Seizing on the first available sight, he said, "See that perfectly symmetrical hill up ahead, the one shaped like a Chinese pointed hat? That's a cinder cone left over from a long time back. Lots of volcanic activity around these parts a couple thousand years ago."

"Did you say a couple *thousand* years ago?"

"Sure did."

"Then I don't have to worry about one of these mountains erupting this afternoon?"

"Probably not, but if you hear a big rumbling sound, get ready to run. You never know."

"You're kidding."

"Yeah, I'm kidding."

"That's good. This is such rugged country that I wouldn't even know which way to run—and I sure wouldn't want to be lost out here."

"Neither would I. However"—he made a sweeping gesture to indicate the line of snowcapped mountains to the west—"the Cascades over there would give you a point of reference that'd be hard to miss."

"You like geology, don't you?"

"My minor in college. I majored in biology. Found out I liked animals a little better than rocks."

"And just where did you make this discovery?"

"At Berkeley."

"Berkeley? I don't associate Berkeley with ... well—"

Brian laughed. "Go on, say it. You don't associate Berkeley with a rural vet who wears cowboy boots?"

"Something like that."

"Berkeley was back a few years, but if I look around long enough, maybe I can unearth a few headbands and even a guitar to show you."

"It's a long way from headbands and a guitar at Berkeley to a veterinary practice in Silver Pine. How'd that happen?"

"Doesn't everybody change majors a few times?"

Tory shook her head. "Not me. International business at the University of Washington from day one."

"Oh, come on. You must have thought about a different major somewhere along the line."

"I always knew I'd be joining NFM right out of college, so that's what I prepared for."

"Did your preparation match your interests?"

"With a family business to consider, that was beside the point."

"But with your life to consider, it's the whole point, isn't it?"

"Not really. I wasn't going to make a living painting watercolors."

"Ah ... but you wanted to."

She didn't answer, and Brian suspected she was thinking back to an earlier time. He watched her hands tighten around the hat she was holding in her lap. Finally she said in a low voice, "It wouldn't have been ... acceptable."

"Do you still paint?"

"Not for years. It takes too much time."

"Who says?" he asked rhetorically, liking her uptight father less and less as Tory seemed to retreat into a somber mood again. No wonder she thought making money was the most important thing in life. Apparently that was what her workaholic father had preached to her. Brian's attempt to tease her had apparently stirred up some unpleasant memories. Time to change the subject again. "So, you really want to know how I got from Berkeley to Silver Pine?" he asked.

She brightened and said, "I certainly do."

"Well, it was a round trip, from here to there and back. I grew up on a ranch north of here—the Running K up near High Desert. Matter of fact, you flew right over the place on your way in. My folks wanted me to go to college all right, but they were thinking more of the agriculture program at OSU. Drove 'em crazy when I came up with that scholarship to Berkeley, but . . . well, it seemed like a good idea at the time. I'd had about enough of cows and sagebrush to last me, or so I thought."

"A geology scholarship . . . or biology?"

"Either one would make some sense anyway, but, no, it was in writing."

"Writing? Dr. Rafferty, you are a man of many talents."

"Let's just say I had an enthusiastic English teacher who encouraged me, made sure I sent in all the right applications. Yeah, Mrs. Bourdreau had me convinced I was going to write the 'Great American Novel' someday."

"Let me get this straight. You got a writing scholarship to Berkeley, where you somehow got sidetracked into majoring in biology, minoring in geology, and now you're back here as a veterinarian?''

"Sort of a roundabout trip, wasn't it?''

"What happened to your writing? Did you come up with the 'Great American Novel'?''

"Not yet.''

"But you still write?''

"Oh, yeah. Different stuff though.'' He didn't go into detail right now about some of his current writing, especially the essays on land-use planning.

"Then—''

"How did I end up back here? Well, in my junior year of college, I was hanging out at coffeehouses listening to depressing poetry that seemed go nowhere— you know the type—and finally I just got fed up. Or maybe I grew up. I came home that summer to work on the ranch and the next thing I knew, I was applying to the College of Veterinary Science at Washington State.''

"And . . . what was her name . . . Monica?''

"Yes, Monica.'' Brian hesitated and then shrugged. He might as well finish the story. "She liked the depressing poetry better. The coffeehouses and that whole self-conscious artistic scene—red slashes across canvas that are supposed to represent God, or cosmic reality, or maybe Mickey Mouse's secret obsession. I don't know. Oops. I hope that's not the kind of watercolor you do . . . or did.''

"Don't worry. What I used to paint, you could actually recognize.''

Brian continued, determined to get this out and done. "Monica liked the idea of seeing me as a struggling author in the south of France or something, with her draped artistically over the typewriter, I guess. But . . .

that wasn't for me. I think I was supposed to write just enough of that depressing poetry I mentioned to qualify me as a tortured, but interesting, artist she could show off while we visited friends on their yachts in the Mediterranean.''

Tory laughed at his account. ''I think I know a few people in Seattle Monica might enjoy, but forgive me if I say that you don't seem to fit in with the group.''

''You're right. That was a problem.''

''So, if you no longer write depressing poetry, or novels, what do you write?''

He cocked an eyebrow at her. ''Now I write about whatever I want . . . about helping a cow give birth, the local geology, being a part of this community, and . . . and whatever else comes to mind. I like living here . . . and I write how it feels to live in a place I like. Sounds kind of tame, but I'm able to do the veterinary work I love and write, too. Maybe I'll become the Oregon version of James Herriot.''

''And Monica didn't see herself as the Oregon version of Mrs. Herriot?''

''No. Monica most definitely did not like that idea. No yachts or ascots here in Silver Pine. She . . . well, it just wasn't going to work.'' He thought, but did not add, that Monica would never be happy without a country club nearby, or fabulous shopping, or large amounts of money. Being with him hadn't been enough. And how painful that realization had been for him. He sat silently, wondering how he had managed to go from one conversational minefield to another. A moment later he was grateful when Tory apparently recognized his embarrassment and tried to lighten the mood.

"You don't mean to say she even passed up the pet parade?"

With relief, Brian matched her playful tone. "Yes, she did. Hard to believe, but true. You'll see for yourself Monday what a stellar event that is. You're planning to go, aren't you?"

"Not only am I planning to go, but Jake apparently has a starring role."

"I guess that means that Amy and Darla talked to you."

"Now how on earth would you know that?"

"Let's just say that I have my secret sources—all that time spent deciphering esoteric poetry wasn't completely wasted on me. I know how to read clues . . . and besides, they borrowed Jake last year."

They lapsed into a companionable silence and watched the wilderness unfold ahead of them. As he drove, Brian automatically noted the snowpack still remaining on the mountains. The drought of the past several years had given way this past spring to heavy precipitation, leaving the area beautifully green and re-energizing the efforts to develop the NorthPointe ski resort. Brian preferred to do his skiing up at the nearby Martin's Hill area, constructed locally by area residents in the fifties. There, he and his friends could hike in on snowshoes, use the ancient rope tow, and generally rough it. A small warming hut made of logs provided the only touch of comfort. Not for him the Aspen culture in which Monica had thrived, where the biggest challenge seemed to involve wearing the most outrageous outfit on the slopes—or possibly drinking the most in the bars each evening. Monica had loved Aspen for all the reasons he had disliked it. He remembered one particularly sharp exchange they had had at Aspen, shortly before the termination of their engagement.

"Can't you just pretend to have a good time?" she had snapped.

"You aren't seriously telling me that Arturo and Yvonne and those other clowns are saying anything worth listening to, are you?"

"Who cares whether they're worth listening to? They're *fun*. Don't you know how to have fun?"

"Yes, I do. But it doesn't involve endless gossip interrupted only by passionate discussions of ski fashions."

"Oh, and it's better to sit at the edge of a mosquito-infested lake waiting breathlessly for the first sighting of a damned blue heron or something?"

"I'd say so."

"You're impossible, Brian. You don't even try to like normal things."

"Maybe your idea and my idea of normal don't overlap enough."

Monica was probably snorkeling off the Caymans, or trekking through Kenya in a designer safari outfit by now. Wherever she was, Brian knew she was having a marvelous time enlivening the cocktail hour conversation with hilarious tales of her near-disastrous alliance with the hick from Oregon.

But today was a day that this hick intended to enjoy the pleasures of Oregon, Brian thought. He deliberately passed by the sign indicating the nicely manicured Rattlesnake Butte State Park, preferring to pull to the side of the road at a barely marked track a mile or so beyond.

"This is the picnic area?" Tory asked, puzzled.

"My picnic area anyway. Better view of Fish Lake

and Tumbledown Mountain from here, and no damned tourists. Do you mind a little walk?''

''That depends,'' she said. ''Just why was that park we passed named 'Rattlesnake Butte'?''

''Don't worry. That's a geologic term referring to a certain kind of rock formation. Even if there were any live rattlesnakes around—and this is a little high for them, so I don't think there are—they wouldn't bother you unless you bothered them.''

''I'm certainly glad to hear that, but in case any of them are listening, I'd like to go on record as saying that I promise not to bother them at all.''

''So you don't mind a walk?''

''I'd love one. This air seems to invigorate me. And,'' she added, ''I can see why you didn't want to stop at the state park. This whole area is absolutely overrun with tourists. Why, we must have seen three cars in the past half hour.''

He slung the basket out of the truck easily and led the way through a profusion of wildflowers up over a rise and along a faint, dusty trail. ''See this green ground cover with leaves that look like miniature holly? That's kinnikinnick. Grows all over like a carpet. If you'd been here a month earlier, you could have seen the bitterbrush in bloom. It's worth seeing—yellow blossoms along the road for miles.''

''How'd you ever find this in the first place?''

''Game trail,'' he explained. ''I guess the local deer like the same scenery I do. Can you make it up this slope? One of my favorite views coming up.'' He put out a hand. It wasn't that tough a climb for him in his boots, but Tory was making do with some tennis shoes that weren't exactly designed for this terrain. Besides, he'd take any excuse to get close to her.

She accepted his offer of help, slipping slightly on the loose rocks. "Thanks," she said. "This is a little harder than walking along the Seattle waterfront." As they topped the hill, Brian could tell from the look on her face that she understood why he had wanted her to see the view. Ahead of them lay Fish Lake, quiet and serene, while behind it Tumbledown Mountain stood guard over the grassy area leading to the lake. The origin of the mountain's name was immediately apparent from the rugged gray stones trailing down its flank.

"There's an even bigger lake beyond, one that borders the state park, but I like this place better because you can't get here by road. Keeps it more private."

"It's spectacular. I can see why you love it."

"There's a lot more scenery where that came from. What's your pleasure? Hike or eat first?"

"Eat, for sure. I don't know what's come over me since I've been here, but I'm ravenous all the time."

"Aunt Sarah's cooking probably has something to do with that. I react to her food the same way."

Brian opened the basket and exclaimed, "Ah, she does love me." He lifted out the packet of sandwiches and offered one to Tory. "Ham and swiss on rye."

"I suppose she made the cheese herself," Tory asked.

"You think you're kidding," Brian said, "but I wouldn't be surprised. I know for sure she made the bread. That's her caraway dark rye. Wins a blue ribbon at the Howard County fair every year. You'll get samples when she gears up for that."

"When is it?" she asked, grasping the overflowing

sandwich firmly in both hands before taking a delicate bite.

"Early August."

"Oh, well . . . I'll probably miss it then, but . . . this sandwich is certainly delicious."

Brian took heart from the fact that she hadn't said for sure that she'd be gone by then, and he hoped it wasn't his imagination that she seemed to be studying her sandwich more carefully than necessary. Were her cheeks a bit redder than they had been a minute ago? Maybe. He plunged in. "Say, I know you're anxious to get back to your company and all, but is there any special reason you can't stay around Silver Pine a little longer? Plenty more beautiful country I could show you."

"Lots of reasons, and every one of them has a dollar sign attached."

"But everybody needs a break from work—"

"—and if I take one, my clients will find someone who doesn't. It's been hard enough convincing some of them that I'm old enough and competent enough to manage their affairs. My father built NFM from the ground up, and it's my responsibility to take care of it."

"And what about you?"

"What about me?"

"Is that all you want? To take care of NFM?"

"Of course not. I want lots of things besides that, but first things first. That means NFM."

"And no time to paint."

"That's right. No time to paint, at least not right now."

Brian handed over a brown crockery container of pickles. "Dill. Sarah wins prizes for these too. Crunchy as all get out." He tried for a casual tone as he finally got around to the question he'd been wanting to ask all day. "When you do get away from NFM, assuming you ever do, is there some guy waiting outside the door?"

"Sure, sometimes."

"I mean, is there some special guy?"

"Not really," she answered.

"I guess it'd be tough playing second fiddle to a dollar sign," he said, wadding up the waxed paper from his sandwich.

"No worse than playing second fiddle to a cow in labor," she said.

"Touché."

"So?" At last she was looking directly at him. "How about you? Are you seeing someone special?"

"No." The single word, quietly emphatic, seemed to hang between them in the air for a long time. Before Brian could act on his next impulse and reach for her, Tory broke the spell.

"Maybe we could go for that walk now."

"Whatever you say. Rafferty Tours at your service."

The next several hours passed much too quickly for Brian's taste. Tory was a good sport as she scrambled over rocks and up the trails that he had tramped for years. Whenever they'd stop to look out at the wilderness that stretched away to the horizon, she appeared to be enjoying the scenery as much as he did, if not more. Surely someone who could appreciate this kind of an afternoon wouldn't really want to sell her house and land to a corporation with no interest in the natural beauty and tranquillity of the area. She might think she was a city girl, content to be surrounded with her faxes and power lunches and dollar signs, but her enthusiastic reaction to this afternoon's walk gave evidence that there was a different side to her, a softer side. At least that was the way it seemed to someone looking for such evidence, Brian thought. Maybe he was just fooling himself. After all, he had been wrong about Monica, but still . . .

By the time they had returned to the picnic basket and demolished the juicy peaches and homemade chocolate chip cookies that completed Sarah's picnic lunch, Brian had no doubt that he wanted to spend more time with Tory, a lot more time. His conscience still nagged at him over that hasty promise, but he'd talk to Sarah and get released from it the minute they returned to town.

"Funny. I thought chocolate chip cookies were just for kids," Tory said. She licked the last of the chocolate, now melted in the afternoon's heat, from her fingers. "Was I ever wrong. These are great."

"I don't know that I can come up to Sarah's standard," Brian said, "but I make a pretty fair yellow chicken curry, if you're interested in coming over to my place for dinner tonight."

"East Indian cuisine?" Tory asked.

"Thai, actually."

"Where'd you learn to do that?"

"My Berkeley days weren't spent entirely in quaint little coffeehouses. I worked at a Thai restaurant all through college. I ate well and picked up some good recipes along the way."

"Well, I suppose Sarah might be getting a bit tired of feeding me—"

"No way. She'd feed you five meals a day and be happy."

"Just the same, she's done more than her share. I

don't know about the other Saturday night possibilities for food in Silver Pine.''

"Burger and fries at the Shack or chicken-fried steak at Bennett's.''

"That's what I thought. Your yellow chicken curry sounds terrific. I accept.''

"Good. How spicy do you like your food?''

"How spicy can you make it?''

"A challenge, eh? Let's go.'' Now that he knew he'd be spending the evening with Tory, Brian lost his reluctance to start for home.

They found the truck where they had left it, but now a Howard County sheriff's patrol car was parked nearby and Brian recognized Mike Bonner standing beside it, notebook in hand.

"Hey, I was just writing you a note. Figured you'd be along sooner or later.''

"Hi, Mike. Trouble?'' Brian said.

"Garnett over at Forty-Mile was looking for you. One of his mares tangled with a barbed-wire fence pretty good and he wants you over there pronto.'' Mike looked pointedly at Tory until Brian performed a hasty introduction and then continued. "Cindy called Sarah and Sarah called me. She knew you were heading up this way, so I just looked for the truck. Wouldn't want you to have an empty Saturday afternoon.''

"Thanks a lot,'' Brian said.

"Any food left?'' Mike asked. "Sarah said she packed a lot.''

Brian pulled out an extra sandwich out and tossed it to him. "This ought to hold you.''

"Jackpot . . . rye bread. Any cookies left? No? Too

bad. Well, pleased to meet you, Tory. I'll radio in that you're on your way, Brian.''

Brian turned to Tory. "Well, that kills the dinner party. Forty-Mile is a ways from here. Rain check till tomorrow night?''

"Sure. Probably just as well anyway. I still have all that work I skipped out on today. My two-footed clients aren't getting nearly the personalized service from me this weekend that your four-footed ones are from you.''

Chapter Five

A soft whining nearby brought Tory partway out of her deep sleep. Thinking she must have dreamed it, she turned over and nestled back under the warm quilt. Again came the insistent sound—and she whirled around to see two warm brown eyes staring at her over the side of the bed. ''Jake! I'd forgotten you were here.'' The whining intensified and was now accompanied by frantic gyrations of the dog's tail. ''What time . . . ? Never mind . . . doesn't matter. I guess you're telling me you want to go out.'' Barefooted, she followed the now-galloping dog down the staircase and out the front door. Her sleep had been so complete, her dreams so vivid, that it took her a minute to orient herself in the warm, sun-filled morning. Stepping out onto the porch, she reconstructed the events following yesterday's picnic.

After a rapid trip back to Silver Pine, Brian had dropped her off with a hasty farewell, seemingly already preoccupied with the injured horse he needed to tend. He'd hesitated before leaving, his tanned arm resting on the open window of the pickup. After starting several times to speak, at length he shrugged his shoulders and said, with a wry smile, ''Ah, nuts! It'll hold till tomorrow. Back as soon as I can make it,'' and he was off.

While watching the brake lights from his truck glow red as he slowed for the corner, Tory asked Jake, ''What was that all about? Guess we've been stood up in favor of a big old horse. I don't know about you, but that's a first for me. So . . . would you care to dine with me tonight? You have your choice of dog food or dog food.'' Jake wagged his tail and followed her through the door. Once inside, he led the way straight to the tall kitchen cupboard that contained an open forty-pound sack of dog food. ''Been here before a few times, haven't you?'' she inquired, stroking his silky head. ''Well, it's nice to have the company.'' Later, Jake followed her upstairs to flop on the braided rug at the side of her bed as though he'd been doing it all his life. No wonder people liked having dogs around, she thought as she drifted off to sleep.

Coming back to the present, Tory leaned on the porch rail and surveyed her property. What with one thing and another, she hadn't even taken the time to walk all the way around the house and yard yet, but she could do that today. Taking a deep breath and reveling in the sweetness of the air, she realized that even the act of breathing felt different here, more like a positive pleasure than something she did automatically, just to get air into her lungs. So this was a summer Sunday morning in a small town. ''It's great!'' she announced out loud, surprising both herself and Jake, who was climbing the steps after completing a circuit of the yard. He crowded close to her legs, then danced back down the steps, as though urging her to walk with him. Tory laughed, a joyous, free sound. ''How could I ever have been afraid of you? Okay, let's explore. Just let me get some clothes on.''

As she reentered the house, she glanced into the dining room and saw the papers still piled haphazardly next to her laptop on the table. That wasn't like her, to leave things in such a mess. Then she remembered her hasty leavetaking yesterday morning. Was it only yesterday that she had let the sound of someone chopping wood—like a rural Pied Piper—lure her from her work? The drive, the picnic . . . Brian.

She brought herself sharply back to reality. Okay, but that was yesterday, and Brian wasn't the only one with responsibilities. She had things to do, and today she would do them . . . but just not quite yet. Right now Jake was waiting, but she promised herself that she'd get to work immediately following a grand tour of the yard. She knew from experience that she'd better not check her messages on the cell phone before going back outside. If she dared to let her mind focus on the work-related decisions, problems, and questions that probably awaited her, she'd never get out the door. Better to explore the yard first. Maybe she could make that her new motto: Play first, then work—if you feel like it. She shook her head at her newfound frivolity, knowing what her father would have said to a work ethic like that. ''What's the matter with you, Tory? Work comes first, always. You know that.'' She used to believe that, but who other than her father could resist a walk outside on a morning like this?

A decaying brick walk, with grass growing up through the spaces between the faded red blocks, led around the side of the house and past numerous rosebushes, whose fragrance permeated the air in spite of their neglected state. Tory literally had to push aside a large-leafed hydrangea bush with blue-gray flowers to reach the back porch of the house. She faced away from the door and looked out, much as Ellen must have when taking a break from her kitchen duties. Nearby was a low rock wall surrounding plants that had ceramic tags affixed to them. Stepping over the barrier, she read some of the labels: *Summer Savory, Rosemary, Tansy, Sweet Basil.* An old-fashioned herb garden, placed close to the kitchen door so that dinner preparations could be interrupted long enough for someone to make a quick run to get a fresh sprig of this or a few leaves of that. Tory crumbled a dusty green leaf between her fingers and smelled, even before reading the tag, that this was a sage plant.

She stepped back out of the enclosed space and followed the brick walk as it meandered away from the house. Ahead, a trellis alive with pink climbing roses formed an arch over the walk. On closer inspection, Tory could see that its white paint was flaking and its uprights had begun to sag to the side. Listening to the hum of bees as they occupied themselves in the surrounding flowers, she ventured farther until she found an inviting stone bench on which to sit and look back toward the house. Jake explored the shrubbery, startling a covey of quail into a hasty retreat from the garden toward what appeared to be a small barn or shop of some kind. If she felt just a little more ambitious, she'd walk back and take a look at it, but she felt so relaxed and peaceful just sitting here. Maybe later. When she closed her eyes, she could hear the distant rush of the river, or was that the wind in the trees? It didn't really matter. This was a beautiful sanctuary, laid out with care and love. Unfortunately it, like the house, had been neglected for some time, probably since her aunt's death.

Still, even now it remained a valuable property. Judging from the amount that the California Development Corporation had offered her for it, no doubt they had every intention of investing considerable money to restore the house to elegance. That thought cheered her a little, but Tory still felt a small stir of disquiet at the notion that this lovely oasis would soon become a corporate sales office. It seemed such a cold, impersonal use for what had once been a much-loved family home. *Get a grip, Tory,* she admonished herself. *You're not going to live here, so why not let them fix it up and take care of it? Besides, have you suddenly developed an aversion to making money?*

With reluctance, she finally stood and meandered back toward the house—her house, at least for now. She had been daydreaming too long, and daydreams didn't bring in clients. She had work to do.

Hours of concentrated work had yielded considerable progress, and with a final click of the mouse, Tory logged off her computer. She rolled her shoulders to ease the strain and then leaned back in her chair, satisfied. It was still early afternoon. For a Sunday, that wasn't bad, compared to her usual routine. While most people thought of weekends as vacation days, Tory merely slowed down to eight-hour workdays. Now she had only to return the calls on her cell phone before she could count herself finished for the day. *Only!* Judging from the number of calls awaiting her attention, apparently most of her clients didn't take weekends off either.

She disposed of several matters with quick instructions to her secretary via voice mail and considered the rest. C. J. Sheffield could wait. Though she always looked forward to their meetings, he'd be out with his family on their sailboat in the San Juans over the long weekend anyway. He was one of her few big clients who insisted on saving his weekends for friends and family. Laura Grantley merely wanted to confirm an appointment. Art Sutter wondered whether to buy more technology stocks or tilt his portfolio toward international offerings. He must have been talking to his son-in-law again.

Carson had left several messages, each one proposing a different activity for the coming week. Tory dialed his number, guiltily aware that she would have to be more direct with him in order to make it clear that they truly had no romantic future together. He was fun, but they would never be more than friends. With more impatience than usual, she waited through the annoying words of his answering machine message—"Here's listening to you, kid!"—before speaking. Maybe he'd be more attractive if he changed that silly message. She wondered idly what kind of a message Brian would put on an answering machine, assuming he even owned one. She wasn't sure any machine could provide more information than the ever-perky Cindy and the highly efficient Silver Pine grapevine. At the series of beeps that finally signaled her chance to talk, she said, "Hi, Carson. It's Tory. Thanks for the calls, but I really don't think you should count on me for anything in the next few days.

I'm going to be pretty well tied up with this Silver Pine business for . . . for longer than I'd thought. Have a great Fourth of July.'' She deposited the phone on top of the stack of completed work. There. That ought to hold him until they could talk face-to-face.

Just as she stood up, the telephone on the hall table began to ring. Was Brian back?

"Miss Baxter? Tory?'' The cheerful voice on the phone was instantly recognizable. The last time Tory had heard it, barking dogs had provided background music. "This is Cindy . . . you know, from Dr. Rafferty's office?''

"Yes, I remember. Hello.''

"Brian asked Fred—that's Fred Kalek from Forty-Mile, you know—to give me a message for you. See, Fred was over to the Garnett ranch yesterday . . . where Brian was taking care of that mare, you know?''

"Yes.''

"And she's doing fine.''

"That's—''

"And Fred had to come to Silver Pine today for feed—I work at the feed store weekends, you know—so Brian asked Fred to tell me to tell you he wouldn't be back in town till real late tonight, or maybe even tomorrow morning. Sort of confusing, but Brian wrote down the exact message.'' There was the sound of shuffling paper, and then she read: " 'Sunday dinner won't work. Can you wait until Monday to burn your tongue?' '' Cindy detoured from her task of delivering the message long enough to add her own editorial comments. "Guess that means he's fixing you Thai food. You're braver than most of us. So, how about Monday?

Fred's standing here right now, so he can take the message back with him.''

Tory smiled at the idea that half of Howard County knew about her dinner plans, right down to the menu. She stifled a wild urge to ask Cindy whether Fred approved of her having dinner Monday with Brian. ''Sure, tell Fred to tell Brian that Monday will be fine.''

''Okay, will do.''

''And, Cindy, thanks for relaying the message.''

''No problem. See you at the parade tomorrow. I hear Amy and Darla are borrowing Jake.''

''Well, Jake's not really my dog.''

''Near enough to count, the way I hear it. You'll go to the parade to see him, won't you? Amy said—''

''Wouldn't miss it for the world,'' she said, thinking, not for the first time, that she'd hate to try keeping a secret in this place. Still smiling, she hung up the receiver. What a funny, friendly place, and it seemed to be having the strangest effect on her. Even if Brian wouldn't be back for dinner, she wasn't in the mood for another round of office work this afternoon. The people in her office would be shocked. The hard-driving Tory Baxter, not in the mood for work? Ridiculous. *Really, Tory—usually you don't have enough time for anything but work, and now you want to spend the day wandering around some old house in Silver Pine dreaming about a horse doctor you'd never met until two days ago? Ridiculous.* What was going on here? As Tory tried to imagine her father's reaction to this carefree attitude, ''Ridiculous!'' echoed again through her head. Ridiculous to get a dog, ridiculous to take a Saturday-afternoon drive when there was work to be done, ridiculous to consider that such work might not be the most important thing in a person's life.

As though a curtain into the past had parted, Tory remembered other times from her childhood when her father had labeled things ridiculous. Ridiculous to use precious time during business hours to attend Tory's ballet recital, or her school conference, or to view her fifth-grade watercolor entry in a school art show. "If I don't go to work, who'll pay for those expensive lessons?" he'd challenged her mother. Funny how Tory could hear his voice clearly in retrospect, but her mother's replies seemed muted, soft and muffled—like her mother herself. Never one to call attention to herself, she had dried Tory's tears and attended Tory's performances alone. Tory remembered that her mother had always been there, but she also remembered that she had not especially prized her mother's presence. Tory had been too busy looking over her mother's shoulder, hoping that her busy, successful father would come to see her accomplishments. It rarely happened, and eventually Tory learned to look down on her mother for always being so available, for having a life so devoid of important matters that she was able to attend Tory's childish little recitals.

Jake's insistent nuzzling of her hand brought Tory back to the present. "Time to go out again, boy? You're getting pretty demanding." In her father's world, there had been no dirt, no dogs, no wasted time . . . and, she acknowledged at last, very little emotion. She let Jake out the door, closed it thoughtfully, and turned to face her new home. Some people had trouble reading market trends and the Nasdaq composite index, but they were a snap for Tory next to the unfamiliar territory she had entered . . . the territory in which people and emotions took precedence over work. Maybe it was time she learned some more about her father's childhood. Somewhere in his brother's house she might find clues to explain her father's distaste for Silver Pine and his unwillingness to talk about his boyhood here. She moved purposefully toward the hitherto unexplored back part of the house.

Beyond the dining room, sliding doors opened into a small back room—probably a back parlor originally—that her uncle had converted into a makeshift bedroom in more recent times. Obviously, this had been the room her uncle had lived in most of the time after his wife had died. It was cluttered with everyday things, the possessions of someone who no longer cared about his immediate surroundings. A narrow cot hugged one wall. Beside it stood a gooseneck lamp on a rickety card table, which also held a set of reading glasses, some newspapers, and a silver-framed picture of a young woman laughing over her shoulder. What had Sarah said the other night? "Jim lost heart after Ellen died. That beautiful house he built specially for her just sat there—with him living in one little part of it once she was gone." Tory could almost see him moving back and forth between this room and the nearby kitchen, bypassing the front parlor with the two large, comfortable chairs flanking the massive fireplace with the intricately carved mantel, or the dining room table that could accommodate twelve but still contained two chairs set cozily together at one end.

Unbidden, a picture of her childhood apartment flashed into her mind—her father at one end of the sleek glass table and her mother at the other, with Tory in the middle and Marta serving endless silent meals. Funny, Tory hadn't noticed at the time how little contact her parents had. It hadn't seemed unusual then, but now, thinking back on it from an adult perspective, Tory realized that her parents' household—and her parents' marriage—were both quite different from this one. Abstract paintings, not photos, had decorated the apartment where she grew up. Her father had pronounced them good investments, and dismissed as irrelevant her mother's timid comment that she didn't really enjoy them. Tory's own watercolors were never taped to the refrigerator, as she had seen the work of her school friends displayed. Instead, they had been quietly gathered into a private album by her mother. Sometimes on rainy days when her father wasn't home, she and her mother would curl up and look at them together.

No doubt the framed picture on the card table was of the beloved Ellen Tory kept hearing about. She picked it up and carried it over to the window for a better look. Opening the heavy damask curtains and peering closely at the face of her aunt, she smiled involuntarily at the pixie grin before her, but when she tried to remember anything about this aunt, she found a curious void. Had Ellen ever been mentioned in her parents' home? She looked friendly, like a nice aunt to have had, but Tory had no memory to which she could tie her picture. Ellen might as well have existed in another world, not merely another state, all these years.

Across the room from the cot stood a massive rolltop desk and matching chair, a little brass key placed invitingly in the keyhole of the desk. Tory's lifelong habit of minding her own business, encouraged by the formal, reserved atmosphere in which she'd grown up, made her reluctant to intrude on the privacy of others, even now, when she owned all this. Here goes nothing, she thought as she turned the key. The cover of the desk rolled smoothly upward, exposing an orderly interior. All the little pigeonholes across the back were filled with neatly labeled envelopes and papers, everything laid out carefully, as though ready for inspection. Prominently displayed in the very center of the compartment lay a bulky manila envelope with a name written carefully across the outside: *Miss Victoria Baxter.*

A small box, wrapped for mailing in heavy brown paper, was propped in front of the envelope. Like the envelope, the box was addressed to Tory and the return address listed J. S. Baxter, Silver Pine, Oregon. Though the postmark was faint with age, Tory could make out enough numbers to tell that the package had been mailed several months after her birth. Her father's distinctive bold printing marched across the front of the parcel: *Refused—Return to Sender.* The words were underlined twice. The tape holding the package closed had long since lost its adhesive quality, and Tory was able to undo the flaps quickly. Inside the box, a cardboard cylinder stuffed with tissue paper cushioned a solid object.

As the protective layers fell away, a carved teddy bear emerged, marvelously detailed and smooth to the touch. An elaborate coat and hat—complete right down to a row of buttons in front—adorned the child's toy, and the bear's cheerful face was set permanently in a gentle smile. The accompanying card read, *To Baby Victoria with love from Uncle Jim and Aunt Ellen.* A toy to delight a young child, or, indeed, someone of any age.

Tory looked again at the discarded wrapping. ''Refused.'' A baby present to her—and her father had refused it. What could have caused him to behave with such malice toward his only brother? With a mixture of sadness and apprehension, Tory set the bear on the desktop and turned her attention to the large envelope waiting for her.

Someone had hoped that she would come someday to explore this house, to do exactly what she was doing. Tory shivered in spite of the warm air of the summer afternoon. Not knowing what to expect, she sank into the chair in front of the desk and slowly opened the envelope. A packet of pictures spilled out as she pulled from its depths several closely written pages. She put the pictures aside and read:

My dear Victoria,

You don't know me, of course, but I have long wanted to know you. This letter is my explanation for why we have never met or corresponded. I couple it with an apology for the inadvertent harm that I did your father, my younger brother, so long ago. Not knowing what Richard has said about me through the years, I start at something of a disadvantage, but bear with me.

As you almost certainly know, your father and I grew up in Silver Pine, attended Silver Pine High School, and eventually fell in love with the same lovely young woman, Ellen Hargreaves.

Since Richard dated Ellen first (they were in the same class at school, and I was three years older), he always seemed to feel that I "stole" her from him when I returned from college. Indeed, he was so bitter about the situation that I don't think he ever acknowledged that their relationship was doomed long before I returned to town. That is the reason, in brief, that Richard and I never corresponded.

He didn't feel the love for Silver Pine that Ellen and I did. It always seemed to stifle him, and he could hardly wait to get away, first to college and then to Seattle. To be honest, I probably would have stolen Ellen from him if I could have, but I want you to know that I truly believe that they couldn't have made a successful match, even if they had tried. They were too different, and they wanted different things out of life. However, Richard refused to accept this idea as valid.

When Ellen and I married, and for some years afterward, we tried to mend the breach, but Richard refused our efforts, going so far as to threaten legal action if I continued to write to him. He made me promise never to contact him, or you, for the rest of my life. He even extracted the promise that if he died first, as was the case, I should not attend his funeral. All his requests I have honored—out of sorrow for the unintentional pain Ellen and I caused him, and out of love for my only brother.

I've spent years wondering how much of Richard's seeming inability to be happy was my fault, and I still don't know the answer. While I always loved the slow pace of life in Silver Pine, the friendliness and the simplicity, Richard chafed at everything about it—except Ellen.

Obviously, I can't blame him for loving Ellen, for she was the most intelligent, beautiful, fun-loving girl Silver Pine ever knew. I don't know why she chose me for her husband when she could have had her pick of half a dozen men in town, but I've thanked God for many years that she did.

Dearest Victoria, you are probably wondering by now why I am telling you all this. Since I was unable—knowing Richard's feelings—to be a satisfactory uncle to you during my lifetime, I have had to take a rather roundabout method of trying to bring our family back together at this late date. You wouldn't be reading this letter if I were still alive, so by now you know that I have left you my house and property in Silver Pine. Ellen and I were never blessed with children of our own, so we always intended this house to go to you—along with our love. Please accept it in the spirit in which it is offered, along with my most solemn assurance that Ellen and I never meant to do your father harm.

One more thing before I close. My dog, Jake. He's a wonderful companion and I'd be honored if you would allow him to live with you. My longtime friend and neighbor, Sarah Rafferty, has said she'll be happy to take him if you are unable or unwilling to do so. I realize that your lifestyle must be hectic, but if you can find a place in your life for Jake, you'll never regret it.

With love,
Uncle Jim

P.S. How I wish we could have known you!

Tory saw through moist eyes that the letter was dated May of this year. Perhaps her uncle had suspected that his health was failing. She picked up the faded black-

and-white snapshots and leafed through them. One showed her ecstatic young uncle holding up a fish on a pole while her father looked on from a careful distance. Another caught her uncle and aunt laughing together on the porch of this house. The last picture was one she had seen before, in Seattle. It showed her father, serious in cap and gown, at his high school graduation. There was also a yellowed clipping from the *Seattle Post-Intelligencer* announcing the formation of Northwest Financial Management Group by her father, with a formal picture of him in suit and tie above it.

Just then, Sarah's voice came from the front of the house. "Tory, are you here?"

With the disoriented sensation of waking from a dream, Tory put down the photos and made her way through the dining room into the entryway. "Hi, Sarah. Come on in," she added unnecessarily.

Sarah had already walked into the kitchen to set down the Tupperware bowl she was carrying. She turned to Tory with a frown on her normally cheerful face, "You know, dear, I wouldn't want to meddle—"

"Of course not." Tory answered, trying to keep a straight face.

"—but something has been bothering me today and I really felt I needed to say something to you, even though, strictly speaking, it's none of my business." She gestured toward the bowl she had just deposited on the counter. "Oh, here, before I forget."

"Sarah, not more food?"

"It's nothing—just some coleslaw I make a special way. In this heat I didn't think you'd want much and I heard that Brian wouldn't be getting back tonight."

Again Tory smiled at the lightning speed with which

news traveled in Silver Pine. No, certainly no one around here would ever think of paying undue attention to anyone else's affairs.

"You do like pecans, don't you?" Sarah lowered her voice, as though recipe spies might be lurking in the front parlor. Tory didn't bother to answer, as Sarah seemed quite able to carry on the conversation without any help. "That's the secret . . . pecans . . . and a dash of curry powder. I discovered the curry by accident one time when I grabbed it instead of the paprika—and I've been winning prizes with it ever since."

"Sounds—"

"There's some buttermilk biscuits to go with it, and . . . this!" Sarah reached into her apron pocket and brought forth with a flourish a perfectly ripe tomato. "There you go. From my garden . . . and *this* tomato won't taste like that cardboard the stores try to sell you."

"Sarah, you're just too much," Tory exclaimed. "Whatever would I do without you? Can you stay and help me eat this?"

"No, no, I've got a meeting later with my Four-H cooking club. They're called the Cookie Monsters and the name really fits that crazy bunch. They're baking tonight so we can sell some things tomorrow at the parade for a fund-raiser."

"Do you ever get out of the kitchen?"

"Not much, but then why would I want to? Well, got to go now."

"Sarah, you said you wanted to talk to me about something."

"Where's my head today? 'Course I did, but I clean forgot once I got to talking about everything else. It's about Brian."

"He's all right, isn't he?"

"Well, sure, it's nothing like that. It's just . . . sorry if I seem nosy, but you and Brian seemed to be getting along so well, and I know Brian didn't want anything to mess that up."

"Well, that's good, isn't it?" Tory couldn't understand where this was leading.

"There's something you ought to know."

"Sarah, please tell me whatever it is you want to say. It can't be all that bad."

"I don't want you to prejudge him."

"I won't. I promise." Tory ran through what she knew about Brian, and could find nothing to lead to this nervous hesitation on Sarah's part. But Sarah was pretty old-fashioned, part of a different generation. Maybe she was thinking that Tory would be upset to know that Brian had once been engaged to another girl. That must be it.

Sarah was still struggling. "He wanted to tell you the other day, but it's sort of hard to talk about."

Tory put her out of her misery. "Don't worry, Sarah. He told me all about it."

Sarah looked surprised, and then relieved. "He did?"

"And it doesn't matter to me at all," Tory assured her.

"Oh, Tory, it doesn't? Frankly, I'm surprised. I was afraid you'd think that he was being . . . well, dishonest or something."

"Dishonest?"

"For not mentioning it sooner."

"I only met him Friday, Sarah." Tory found Sarah's evident discomfort refreshing. But then Sarah had probably married her childhood sweetheart and never looked at another man. She didn't realize that people dated a lot more now than they used to in her day. Though Brian's broken engagement was painful to him, it wasn't cause for all this anguish. Trying to reassure Sarah, she said, "Besides, I know that these things happen. People sometimes want different things."

"Exactly. I'm so glad you understand."

"Of course I understand. Sometimes differences can be worked out and sometimes they can't."

"So you talked this all out yesterday, and you're still having dinner together when he gets back?"

"If he can fit it in between medical emergencies."

"Well, then . . . I guess I worried for nothing." Sarah said. "He's really a wonderful person, even if he is my nephew."

Tory laughed. "I believe you."

"Only thing is," Sarah continued, "that rascal wasn't supposed to say anything Saturday. I made him promise not to, didn't want him to spoil things."

"Give him a bad time for breaking his promise if you want, but don't worry about what I think of him," Tory said. "We had a wonderful time."

"Hearing you say that takes a load off my heart, I'll tell you. I'm *so* glad I asked you about it. Now maybe I can enjoy the rest of the day. See you tomorrow at the parade."

"Oh, Sarah?"

Sarah paused with her hand on the doorknob. "Yes?"

"Tell me about the herb garden in back."

"Isn't that a peaceful place? Ellen loved to cook with fresh herbs . . . made quite a study of them. And did you see the little stone bench farther out? Ellen and Jim spent a lot of summer evenings out there."

Tory gestured at the general elegance surrounding them in the hall. "They spent a lot of time in here too, I can see. You'll have to explain this . . . this amazing place to me." Tory placed a hand on the newel post at the bottom of the elaborately carved, golden maple staircase that connected the first and the second stories. She traced the sunburst incised into the wood.

"What about it?" Sarah asked.

"Well, for starters, I've never seen anything like this." She pointed to the bronze figure of a running woman that topped the wooden newel post. Her skirt was blowing in the wind and she had her arms outstretched as though enjoying the heat of a summer day. "Usually a newel post has a simple wooden ball on top."

"Seems to me Jim found this in France on one of their trips. They traveled all over the place, but they always liked Silver Pine best. Anyway, some of these things have lamps sprouting out of their tops, but Jim just wanted the figure. It reminded him of Ellen, so here it is. It does sort of look like her—all happy and relaxed."

"It's beautiful. But it—this whole house—it's like nothing else in Silver Pine. What was he doing?"

"Why, I guess he was making a home for the woman he loved, mostly."

"But it must have taken a fortune to put it together."

"Money never was a problem for Jim, not after collectors and museums started going after his carvings, that is."

"Collectors and museums?"

"How'd you think he earned his living all those years?"

"I . . . I guess I never really thought about it. His

name didn't come up much around our house. I remember hearing he fooled around some with woodcarving—''

Sarah's laugh cut her off. ''Fooled around, eh? That's funny. You telling me with all those museums up in Seattle, you never saw a JSB carving somewhere?''

''JSB? You don't mean—''

Sarah nodded. ''Sure do. You've seen that old barn way out past the herb garden? Well, that's where he worked. At first, he worked here in the house up on the third floor—the ballroom gave him plenty of room to swing a mallet—but the dust and such were something fierce, not to mention carting the wood up and down all those stairs, so he turned the barn into his very own workplace. Ellen'd work in her herb garden or paint— she painted watercolors, you know—and Jim'd work in the barn. Those two weren't far from each other most of the time.''

''Well, of course I've seen JSB carvings. Who hasn't? Why, the Seattle Art Museum has a spectacular JSB waterfall right in the front hall. I don't know how he did it with wood, but you can almost feel the spray coming off it.''

''I know all about that piece,'' Sarah said smugly. ''Watched him work on it some, but I never figured that you wouldn't know about it. Would have mentioned it before if I'd thought. Matter of fact, take a close look at the carving on your mantel over there. It's a miniature of that Seattle piece.''

Tory was stunned by the revelation of her uncle's celebrity status. Whenever Tory's father had mentioned his brother, he always accompanied his words with some disparaging comment about the stick-in-the-mud brother who had stayed behind in Silver Pine. "I can't quite take it in," Tory said. "With all his fame, he still chose to live here, in this little town."

"Why not? He could carve wherever he wanted—and this was home. Besides, Ellen liked it here, and what Ellen liked, Jim liked."

"And the house?"

"Oh, yeah, I forgot . . . you asked about the house a while ago. That started with Ellen way back when they were first married. They honeymooned in San Francisco and she took a fancy to those old houses down there, the way they're fixed up with all kinds of colors and turrets and such. You've probably seen 'em, or pictures of 'em. Anyway, soon as Jim began making money, he started right in to build this house for her. Not another place like it anywhere around these parts. Not many husbands like Jim around either. Jim and Ellen spent a lot of happy years together here. Only thing they wanted that they didn't have was kids. Couldn't, for some reason. Too bad they didn't know you when you were little—they'd have liked that—but they made do by filling in with lots of things around the community. Besides the city council, Jim was on the school board, you know, and they always let kids play in their yard, invited 'em in for tea parties, little Christmas programs up in the ballroom—that kind of thing. Those two made quite a pair."

"And after Ellen died?"

"Sad, isn't it? The neglect, I mean," Sarah said. She brightened as a new thought occurred to her. "But . . . maybe there's a way that this place can be fixed up again. You think that might happen now?"

"I hope so, Sarah. I certainly hope so."

After Sarah left, Tory stood for a long time studying

the intricacies of the mantel in the front parlor. Not only the waterfall, but pine trees and meadow flowers were flung across the expanse over the fireplace in a riot of rural playfulness. Every piece harmonized with its neighbor and fitted into the pattern so smoothly that Tory had passed by this amazing piece of art a number of times without consciously stopping to look at its various parts.

Aside from her surprise at learning about her uncle's fame, she was also in turmoil about her reply to Sarah's parting question. Had she been acknowledging with her answer a truth she hadn't even dared to think to herself yet? Oh, the whole thing was silly. He hadn't even kissed her. She couldn't really be thinking about the possibility of fixing this place up rather than selling it. Or could she? For all the years she'd lived in her apartments in Seattle—first with her parents and now in her own penthouse—she had never felt the sense of being at home the way she did in this house.

Use your brain, Tory, she told herself. *You have a business to run in Seattle.* A small voice answered her— *Yes, and you know as well as you know anything that with the availability of computers and airplanes, you don't have to be in Seattle to run a business there. Think about your uncle, a world-class wood-carver who chose to live here. No more traffic jams, no more loud nightclubs, no more rushing blindly from activity to activity, trying to find the sense of contentment you've found here. There's something so right about Silver Pine, and—you might as well admit it—there's something so right about Brian Rafferty as well.*

After staring unseeing at the waterfall carving on the mantel for some time, Tory roused herself. Time to see the rest of the house. After all, *I may be here for some* time, she thought. Passing the bronze figure on top of the newel post, she said, "Well, Ellen, I'm starting to see why you loved this place so much. You and Jim were richer by far here in Silver Pine than my father ever was—no matter where he was or what his income. Now I'm going to go all the way to the top of this house and really look it over. You don't mind, do you? Didn't think so."

She scampered up the wide staircase, past the master bedroom and along the carpeted hall, pausing to look in turn at the three bedrooms opening off the corridor. Ellen must have had fun with this project. The elaborate furnishings of each room were done in a different color scheme—one in a rose chintz, the next in shades of blue, and the third in buttery yellow tones. The yellow room particularly caught her attention. It had been decorated in a Peter Rabbit motif, and instead of a regular bed, it featured a handmade cradle, ready all these years for the baby Jim and Ellen were never able to have. Like the other bedrooms, it featured a fireplace with a rocking chair pulled up invitingly to one side. On the other side of the fireplace stood an antique wicker baby carriage with outsize wire wheels. It was filled with an assortment of dolls. Next to it nestled a small wooden chair in which sat a ragged white teddy bear missing one eye, a bear that had probably been a much-loved companion of Jim or Ellen as a small child.

Tory brushed aside a few tears as she read the silent message of the room. How strange that she felt such kinship with these people she had never met. She could almost touch their sorrow at not being able to have children, at not being able to know their niece. Sarah had talked casually about Jim and Ellen inviting children for tea parties and Christmas programs, letting them play under the big ponderosas outside. All those things showed that they had tucked their sorrow aside and turned their love for children to good use. When she returned downstairs, she would look at the little carved teddy bear with new appreciation. Ellen and Jim had been admirable people, loving people, and she was proud to be their niece.

Finally, she closed the nursery behind her and continued her tour to the end of the corridor. There, she opened the door that led up a steep flight of steps to the third floor. At the top was another door, which she pushed open with some difficulty to reveal the cavernous ballroom. It was mostly empty. Several trunks and boxes were grouped against one wall, with some folding chairs stacked nearby, possibly waiting for the next neighborhood Christmas program. On a stand in the middle of the room, a full-size carousel horse pranced, its bright colors startling in the gloom. Tory's footsteps echoed and dust swirled in the air as she circled the horse slowly and then made her way past it to the turret alcove.

There, a dust-covered easel stood propped against the windowsill, offering an invitation. The paint pots on the scarred nearby table were dried out, their surfaces a mass of cracks. No paper rested on the abandoned easel, and there were no brushes in evidence, but those were minor matters that could be fixed easily enough. Tory pushed aside the curtains and studied the shades of green visible in the branches of the ponderosa pines etched against the deep blue of the sky. Yes, that scene would do very nicely.

Chapter Six

Darla and Amy clumped across the front porch bright
and early on the Fourth of July, chattering and giggling
with such enthusiasm that Tory didn't need the rasp of
the doorbell to tell her who was there.

"Mom said we couldn't come till now," Darla announced, "but we need time to get Jake ready." She
held up a fistful of bright ribbons and waved at a small
red wagon filled with a variety of stuffed animals.

"Jake's going to pull that?"

"Sure," Darla said. "He'll love it."

"Well, as long as you clear it with Jake."

"We'd show you how much he likes it, but right now
we have work to do. You'll see soon enough." Darla
peered anxiously at Tory, as though fearful she'd been
rude. "Okay?"

"Okay."

"Last year he just walked with us, but this time will

be a lot better. We're going to make him look great. . . . Amy's got a brush and everything. Come on, Jake.''

''What about—'' Amy ventured.

''Oh, yeah. Could we borrow Jake's leash? Sarah said it's in—''

''I know . . . I found it in the cupboard with the dog food,'' Tory said, handing it over. ''Okay, Jake. Good luck.'' The happy trio clattered down the steps, leaving an echo of energy in their wake. When was I ever that excited about a parade? Tory wondered, shaking her head. Then, with a laugh, she answered herself out loud. ''Never—that's when. But I've never been to a Silver Pine Pet Parade before.''

Just then her cell phone rang. Without having to look at her watch, she knew it would be the prearranged call from Marie, her very efficient secretary. Always on time, always available—even at 9:00 A.M. on this Fourth of July morning.

''Good morning, Marie.''

''Good morning, Ms. Baxter.''

''And how are you today?''

''Why . . . I'm just fine, thanks.'' Marie sounded surprised at the personal question. After a slight hesitation, she responded in kind. ''Nice of you to ask. And you?''

''Wonderful . . . couldn't be better. Is it sunny there?''

''Actually, it's overcast right now, with rain due later in the day.''

''I could have guessed. So, what do we need to take care of this fine morning?''

''Let's see . . . Mr. Drummond called—''

''Hold up just a minute. First, how's your son's sore throat?''

"Jeremy's sore throat?" Now Marie sounded posi-
tively astonished, and Tory—remembering the conversation they'd had before she left Seattle—could
understand why. In her haste to get to the airport, Tory
had brushed aside Marie's hesitant protestations that her
son seemed to be coming down sick. With some embarrassment, Tory now recalled her parting comment.
"Look, this trip is an unavoidable nuisance, and I plan
to be back tonight anyway, but if there's any delay, I'll
need you here over the weekend. You'll just have to
make some other arrangements for your child's care."
It was no wonder that Marie was surprised to have Tory
ask about her son's well-being. "Yes, you said he . . .
uh, Jeremy . . . seemed to be getting a sore throat."

"Well, he's feeling a little better, I guess. My husband
took time off work Friday—"

"If he gets sick again, you feel free to take time off
yourself. And there's no need for you to stay at the office
today. After all, it's the Fourth of July. If Jeremy is
feeling better, he'd probably enjoy lighting a few sparklers or something."

"Well, of course he would . . . but you said—"

"I know what I said, but as of now I'm declaring a
new policy. And Marie . . . school conferences. You be
sure to take time for them too. Understand?"

"Conferences. Well . . . yes. Yes, of course. That's
wonderful. Thank you, Ms. Baxter." Marie's voice had
taken on a lilt Tory didn't remember hearing before.

"Okay, now that we have all that straight, what did
Mr. Drummond have to say?" Forcing her mind back to
the business of making money for Mr. Drummond, Tory
picked up her gold Cross pen and started making notes.

*　*　*

Half an hour later, after stuffing the little carved bear into her purse to show Brian, Tory strolled toward the main street of Silver Pine. Memories of a massive traffic jam caused by some long-ago Seattle parade floated through her head. The unavoidable delay in getting to work had roused her father to fury. ''Time lost is money lost,'' he'd growled at his wife when she attempted to calm him. ''And I suppose all the secretaries will take this as license to be late. By God, they'd better not, if they hope to have jobs tomorrow.''

Things were so different here . . . so much slower and more peaceful. She tried to imagine her father growing up in this little town. Was he impatient, even as a child? Did he ever have a pet—or want one? Trying to picture him taking part in this pet parade took more imagination than Tory possessed, but then she realized sadly how very little she knew of his background. He hadn't been the kind of father to take her on his knee and regale her with stories of his childhood. As for her mother . . . well, she had always seemed to be looking anxiously to her husband, whom she adored, for guidance. ''You'll have to ask your father when he comes home. . . . What would your father say? . . . I don't think your father would like that.'' So many negatives, so little joy in their home. Had her mother known about Ellen? Did she ever question her husband about why he wanted to build a life so separate from his boyhood home and his only brother?

While many of Tory's classmates at the exclusive Lafayette Academy went to visit relatives at Thanksgiving and Easter breaks, Tory and her father and mother ate their holiday meals at Seattle restaurants. No fuss, no leftovers, and no awkward encounters with relatives.

Downtown Silver Pine—all four blocks of it—had

been marked off with bright yellow tape to form the parade route, and already people lined both sides of River Street. A surprising number of spectators, children and adults alike, faced north along the flag-draped corridor in smiling anticipation. Tory hadn't realized that Howard County had so many inhabitants, but every one of them seemed to be in town today.

"Tory! Hoo hoo, Tory!" Tory turned to see Sarah standing a few feet away on the corner, surrounded by a knot of young girls holding trays laden with large sugar cookies. On closer inspection, she discovered that the cookies were baked in various animal shapes, and they were leaving the trays at a steady rate. The Cookie Monsters' treasury would get a healthy boost from today's sale.

"Hi, Sarah," Tory said, handing over a dollar to a freckled girl in exchange for a huge chicken-shaped cookie.

"Don't you want a couple of 'Jake' cookies too?" the girl asked. She indicated cookies that, with some imagination, could be identified as golden retrievers. "Amy and Darla might like them."

Tory laughed and handed over two more dollars. "You have a future in marketing, young lady."

Sarah pointed at another cookie on the tray. "I thought maybe you'd want this cow cookie to help you remember your introduction to Silver Pine."

"You people are determined to empty my wallet," Tory said, extracting another dollar. "I won't have any trouble remembering that cow, but this cookie will make a nice memento for Brian."

"He's not likely to forget it either. Where is he?"

"I haven't seen him yet today. Maybe he's not back."

"Oh, he's back. Has to be. He's in charge of this shindig." She waved her hand toward the street. "Probably somewhere down near the start trying to get things organized. Ever try to line up kids and animals?"

"Brian's in charge? He didn't tell me he'd be in the parade."

"Not actually in it. He just sets it up and then watches the fun . . . probably be along directly."

"How long is this parade likely to take?"

"Not too long, maybe fifteen minutes, but they run it around twice, just to make sure you get a good look at everybody."

"You're kidding! Twice?"

"Why not? The parents need time to shoot some pictures—most everybody here is related to someone in it—and the kids love it."

"Makes perfect sense. I've just never heard of such a thing before."

"You've been going to the wrong parades. All those extravaganzas on TV . . . phooey. Just so much fluff and advertising, but *this* is a parade!"

Don Thorne hurried by, clutching a camera. "See you later, Ms. Baxter."

"Yes, of course," she said.

"Good, good." He held up the camera. "Got to get set up. Look for the little redheaded girl on the piebald. My granddaughter."

"Okay," Tory answered, wondering what a piebald was. Tory couldn't remember the last time she'd done anything this simple and fun, but she knew she'd be laughed out of the room by Carson and her other Seattle friends if she tried to describe the sense of contentment she was feeling at this very moment.

"Ms. Baxter?" came a shrill voice from behind Tory. She turned to face an older woman dressed all in white, from high-heeled sandals and pencil-slim pantsuit to a slouch hat pulled down dramatically over one side of her face. She looked ready for a Panama Canal cruise, not a small-town parade. Tory found it hard to avoid staring at the garishly applied makeup, and decided after a second incredulous look that perhaps it would have been better if the woman had pulled the hat down even farther over her features. "Ms. Baxter, we've been so anxious to meet you. I'm Harriet Corcoran and this is my husband, Gil." She gestured back over her shoulder without looking, presumably used to her obedient husband heeling on command.

"Nice to meet you," said the large, florid man standing there.

Tory murmured hello and wondered just where she'd heard of Harriet Corcoran before. Harriet didn't let the silence linger long.

"You don't know us, of course, but Gil here was named to the city council as a temporary replacement for your uncle . . . after his unfortunate death, of course." She shifted smoothly to a sorrowful tone. "So sorry to hear about his passing. We grew up with him, my brother Virgil and I, that is. Went to school with him. Fine man, Jim was." The required expression of condolence delivered, she resumed her strident pitch. "Virgil's on the council too. He and Jim didn't exactly see eye to eye on the future of this town, but Gil here, well, Gil will provide the swing vote on zoning now." Again she pointed back toward her husband, still standing patiently where Tory suspected he spent most of his time, two paces behind his wife. "We'll be here at least until the bank transfers him in November, so don't worry." She lowered her voice and leaned closer. "Plenty of time to get this business done, those changes made, before we leave. I'm so glad to hear that you're more forward-looking than poor Jim was about that property of yours. He just didn't see the potential, did he? All that nonsense about the land trust and such. Now, Virgil has more sense than that. His ranch—where we grew up—well, that place is going to grow more than alfalfa and cows." She winked. "But I guess I don't have to tell you how to make money, not if you're Richard Baxter's daughter."

"Well, I—" Tory hardly knew what to say, but she wasn't required to say anything. Harriet was busily craning her scrawny neck this way and that, looking for someone. Finally waving at a woman on the opposite side of the street, she gave a hasty "Toodle-oo," and teetered off on her high-heeled sandals. Gil trailed dutifully behind.

Alternating between amusement and astonishment at Harriet Corcoran's manner, Tory searched her memory for a clue about where she had heard the name before. Finally, it came to her. At dinner Friday night, Sarah had said something disparaging about Harriet's "la-di-da plans." Somehow, Harriet seemed to think that she and Tory were a lot alike. Now that was something to wonder about!

A ragged drumbeat started up in the distance and everyone turned to watch as four diminutive Cub Scouts in uniform led the parade down the street. With solemn concentration, they carried the American flag and the flag of the state of Oregon past the spectators, working hard to keep more or less in step as they did so. Just behind them came two girls with cats' whiskers painted on their cheeks, smiling and holding up a butcher-paper banner that proclaimed, in wavering green paint, THE FORTY-EIGHTH ANNUAL SILVER PINE PET PARADE. The sign was greeted with applause and cheers on all sides. Tory joined in enthusiastically.

"Like it?" Brian asked, slipping into place beside her.

"Hey, you're back! The parade's wonderful," she replied. "The kids are so cute . . . and everyone's having such a good time."

"As they say, you ain't seen nothin' yet."

For the next ten minutes Tory was treated to the sight of an amazing assortment of pets accompanied by their proud handlers. There were chickens and parakeets in gaily decorated cages, a ferret on a leash, horses with ribbons woven into manes and tails, several unhappy looking goats wearing party hats, cows, sheep, and a pig in a tutu. Interspersed throughout the parade were the dogs—big, little, long, short—dogs of all ages and types. The red, white, and blue of many American flags dominated the colorful display.

She found herself straining like an anxious parent for a glimpse of Jake. Finally, he came into view, his golden fur shiny from his recent brushing. Bright ribbons affixed to his collar fluttered as he trotted along, pulling the now-decorated wagon filled with stuffed animals. Darla and Amy spotted her and steered Jake over closer. Tory held out her arms apologetically, to show she had no camera, but Brian produced one and snapped several quick shots as Jake patiently allowed himself to be posed between his grinning attendants before being swept on in the tide of animals.

Brian pointed out Don Thorne's tiny redheaded granddaughter as she rode by on an enormous black-and-white-spotted horse. So that was a piebald. When Tory remarked in surprise on the little girl's easy confidence, Brian said, "No sweat. She's been on horses since she was three years old."

"Wow! That horse looks pretty big to me."

"Just a matter of getting used to it," Brian answered. "Hey Matt, Matt!" All of a sudden he was waving and calling. "See that kid with the dog in the clown costume? That's Cindy's little brother and his dog, Skipper. I'd like to know how he got Skipper into that outfit."

Everyone who passed seemed to know Brian and he waved and encouraged them all. By the time the parade passed for the second and final time, Tory had clapped and cheered more than she had in a lifetime of watching more elaborate commercial parades.

"Well?" Brian questioned, after the last of the animals had filed by.

"Well what?"

"What did you think?"

"After careful observation," Tory said, lowering her voice conspiratorially, "it is my considered opinion that Jake was the best-looking, best-behaved, most magnificent animal in the parade. Here, have a cookie to celebrate his outstanding performance—and as a reminder of a certain memorable event."

As he accepted the cow-shaped cookie that Tory delivered with a flourish and a wicked grin, Brian found himself relaxing for the first time since he'd left Silver Pine two days ago. Tory really seemed to be enjoying herself here. He had trouble merging the image of this easygoing, smiling woman in the frivolous straw hat with the impatient young sophisticate he'd angered on the road a few days ago. Was it only last Friday they had met? She hadn't been out of his thoughts since. All the way to Forty-Mile and back he'd been calling himself a fool for dreaming that he'd have a chance with her, but she had seemed genuinely glad to see him a few minutes ago, and she was looking up at him now as though he were something special. Maybe he wasn't crazy to be thinking that . . . well, just what was he thinking? He was afraid to put it into words, even to himself. All he knew for sure was that he wasn't prepared to have her walk out of his life after this weekend.

But first things first. He had to tell her about his position on the Silver Pine City Council, and he needed to explain the absurd promise that had kept him from telling her about it before. He should have done it long before this, but at the very least, he had to say something before the scheduled meeting.

"Tory," he began, "I need to talk to you a minute."

"Isn't that what we've been doing?"

"Yes, but"—he nodded to a couple passing by, and gestured along the sidewalk to a place where fewer people stood—"could we get out of this crowd and talk alone?"

"Sure, but I have to make arrangements with the girls about Jake," Tory said, "and then I have this meeting—"

"I know."

"Ah, the infamous local grapevine at work."

"Not exactly. Look, Tory—"

"Oh, and I almost forgot. Is there somewhere around here I can get watercolor paints and paper?"

"Brian! You're back." A petite blonde clutching a strawberry ice-cream cone bounced up to them. "You must be Tory. I'm Cindy ... you know, from the office.''

Tory nodded a greeting.

"Hi, Cindy,'' Brian said. "Yeah, I'm back.''

Cindy apparently found Tory fascinating, but she reluctantly turned her attention back to her boss. "How'd it go?''

"Fine, everything went just fine.''

"Glad to hear it. Barbed wire and horses don't mix too well,'' she said, turning to Tory. "Say, did you see Matt and Skipper today? Matt's my brother,'' she explained, "and Skipper's his dog. He was one unhappy pooch, I'll tell you, when Matt stuffed him into that clown suit. Say, Brian, there's a few things came up since you left. You might want to stop by the office after the meet—''

Brian interrupted her unceremoniously, "Right, Cindy. I'll stop by later. We ... uh ... we have to go now.'' He took Tory firmly by the elbow and steered her away from his surprised receptionist and toward the next corner.

"Brian?'' Tory said as he hurried her along. "What was that all about? Is something wrong?''

"Not exactly,'' Brian said, "but—''

"There you are!'' Darla and Amy cried in unison, after nearly bumping into Brian and Tory as they rounded the corner. Jake still sported his ribbons, but he was no longer hitched to the wagon.

"Wasn't Jake great?'' Amy asked.

Darla chimed in. "Did you see him, Brian?''

"I sure did see him and, yes, he was great,'' Brian said, wondering why there were so many people determined to talk to him at this exact moment. "Tory here was just telling me he was the best pet in the parade."

Tory crouched to pet Jake and speak directly to him. "You were definitely the best pet in the parade."

"I told you he would be," Amy said proudly. "Did you like the way we decorated him . . . the ribbons and all?"

"What can I say?" Brian responded. "He was perfect."

"Absolutely," Tory agreed, "and here's your reward for doing such a good job." She handed them each a cookie.

"Gee, thanks," Amy said. "You didn't have to do that. We didn't expect anything—"

"Hey, look," Darla broke in, delighted. "They're shaped just like Jake . . . same color and everything!"

"I thought you might like them," Tory said. "Besides, I have a favor to ask. Would you mind taking him home for me? I have a meeting right now."

"Hey! Great! Thanks for the cookies."

"And for letting us borrow Jake."

"Anytime," Tory said, giving Jake a final pat. "See you later." Once they were alone again, Tory turned to Brian and smiled. "You were saying . . . ?"

"I was saying—" Brian broke off and alarm bells clanged in his head when he saw Don Thorne approaching. They grew louder when Don spoke.

"Oh, there you are. Starting the meeting without us? Hey, Stu!" he called over Brian's shoulder, and Brian turned to find Stu Merritt approaching from the other direction. "Guess we're ready to start."

Brian knew that the meeting might be ready to start,

but as far as he was concerned, it was already over and done with.

"Start the meeting? I don't understand," Tory said, smiling at Brian.

"Maybe you and Councilman Rafferty have already settled this little business?" Don said with a wink.

Brian could feel the air temperature drop rapidly as the smile faded from Tory's face and she repeated incredulously, "*Councilman* Rafferty?"

"Sure. Brian's been on the city council for . . . what, I guess maybe . . . over a year now. He and Stu are the people you agreed to meet with. Remember, I told you the other day how the council members were split in their opinions about how Silver Pine should be zoned and developed?" He turned in confusion to Brian. "I don't understand, Brian. Didn't you talk to Tory about all this?"

Tory said tonelessly, "Maybe it slipped his mind." She stepped back a pace and fished in her bag for a pair of sunglasses, which she immediately put on.

"Your idea of a little joke, Brian, not telling her you were on the council? Probably didn't want to toot his own horn, Tory, but he does a great job looking after our interests."

"Oh, I'll just bet he does." Tory's answer appeared mild to two of her listeners, but the third one had no trouble picking up the underlying message: *Drop dead, Brian Rafferty.*

Chapter Seven

"**D**id you see my granddaughter? Wasn't she something up on that horse?" Virtually unassisted, Don Thorne kept up a running commentary about the parade as the group made its way through the strolling crowd the short distance along River Street to his office. Fortunately, he was so busy with his own enthusiasm that he didn't seem to notice Tory's lack of response as she walked beside him, keeping as much distance between herself and Brian as possible. Even after they entered the dim office, she kept her sunglasses on.

Through a haze, she vaguely heard and acknowledged the introduction of Stu Merritt, the rather quiet older man with Don. Later, all she could remember was that his horn-rimmed glasses made him look more like her accountant than the third-generation rancher he was. She assumed that he probably contributed more to Silver Pine City Council meetings than he did to their brief encounter, but when she later tried to reconstruct that awful few minutes in the lawyer's office, she realized she had been so focused on the tension between her and Brian that she couldn't remember a single word that Stu Merritt had said.

Behind the concealing dark glasses, she looked with feigned interest from one speaker to the next as they took turns urging her not to sell her property to the California Development Corporation for its NorthPointe office. They produced pictures and charts, and letters supposedly from disgruntled residents near the SouthPointe resort in California. Phrases about "the good of the community," "old-fashioned small-town life," and "a spirit of public enterprise" came and went, distorted and unintelligible to her in her shocked state, like a loudspeaker announcement heard from underwater. Words floated around her while she struggled to assimilate one crucial fact: During all the time they had spent together, Brian hadn't once mentioned his membership on the Silver Pine City Council or this meeting today. The dinner at his aunt's house, the picnic, the drive past the proposed NorthPointe resort—hours and hours when he could have brought up the subject quite naturally—and he didn't do it.

She struggled to admit to herself what logic told her was true. Obviously, it was no accident that he hadn't broached the subject. It had been a calculated move on his part, a deliberate omission for some hidden purpose.

And what had he done instead? He had given her a big rush, put on a false show of interest in her so she would later fall in with his plans for her house and property. The feel of his arms around her as he carried her over the damp ground . . . that walk home in the moonlight, all very convincing . . . and she had fallen for it. Like a silly schoolgirl, she had fallen for it.

She thought back to their first, angry encounter on the road to Silver Pine and contrasted his initial curtness with his conciliatory attitude shortly thereafter outside this very office. How stupid could one woman be? He had flashed that thousand-watt smile, dusted off his "aw-shucks" manner long enough to invite her for a down-home country dinner . . . and she had melted like spring snow on a hot day. He must have had quite a laugh when his country veterinarian act took in the oh-so-sophisticated city girl. And it *had* taken her in. She swallowed hard as the humiliating truth of his betrayal overwhelmed her. She'd been so busy planning a cozy little future with Brian that she'd allowed illusions to cloud her normally cautious approach to the world. For once, she'd let her guard down, and now it was her turn to learn the same bitter lesson her father had absorbed so long ago: Trusting in people—especially people in Silver Pine—could break your heart. Well, he'd learned his lesson, and there was nothing to keep his daughter from doing the same thing. All she wanted at the moment was to get out of this room without breaking down. She absolutely would not give Brian the satisfaction of seeing how thoroughly he'd fooled her. No matter what, she'd leave Silver Pine with her pride intact and then—like her father—she'd never come back.

She rose abruptly to bring the conversation to a close. "Mr. Thorne—"

"Don, call me Don."

"Okay, Don, then. As I see it, there's been no real change in the situation since last week. Thank you for taking the time to set up this meeting, but, frankly, as I warned you then, the town's offer is not in the same ballpark with California Development's proposal, which I intend to accept. As I tried to explain Friday, I have a business to run in Seattle, so I'd like to wrap up this sale as soon as possible.''

"But you don't understand what they're going to do to your place . . . and this town. Stu, Brian, show her . . . tell her. . . .'' He looked to his friends for backing.

"Don, please.'' Tory held up her hand in a "stop'' gesture and shook her head, feeling her throat close and knowing that she'd better get out of the room within the next thirty seconds. Her voice high and tight, she continued, "Simply put, you want to buy my very valuable house and property for considerably less than fair market value in order to make it into a pretty little city park. Lovely sentiment, bad finances. End of discussion. Since you are supposed to be acting as my attorney in this, Don, I'd appreciate it if you would now accept my decision as final.''

"They want to make your property into a parking lot! That's final, all right!'' Brian broke in, unable to contain himself any longer.

Tory continued to look straight at Don and spoke again in the same controlled voice. "I'm sure Dr. Rafferty is being overly dramatic. As he says though, it is *my* property, and I'll do what I think best with it. However, it's apparent that you seem to be in sympathy with his position, Don, so why don't we simplify things and have this sale negotiated by my regular attorney. I'll have him contact you as soon as I get back to Seattle.''

Don drew back stiffly and said, "If that's what you wish, then of course—''

"Yes, that's best. I'm sure of it."

Watching this exchange, Brian felt a wave of despair sweep over him. Now there would be no way to change Tory's mind about selling the property, or about leaving Silver Pine, or about listening to anything he had to say. He cursed himself for the ham-handed way he'd handled things, and for his involuntary outburst. Still, he had to try. If only she'd take off those idiotic dark glasses so he could see her eyes.

"Tory," he began urgently, "if I could talk to you for just a minute—"

"There is nothing more to discuss."

Brian had the feeling she was looking right through him, but he plowed on. "I mean . . . talk outside—"

"There is nothing more to discuss," she repeated.

Don and Stu were looking from Brian to Tory in puzzlement. Brian knew that they sensed a private conversation was in progress, and he wished they would take the hint and leave him alone with Tory. Obviously, she wasn't about to go outside with him. At long last, like an inept actor clumsily responding to a stage cue a couple of seconds late, Don rose from his chair and said, "Stu, let's . . . ah . . ."

Stu jumped up and opened the door. There, he almost bumped into a handsome man, dressed casually in leather jacket and Dockers, entering from the outer office, someone Brian had never seen before.

"Tory!" the man exclaimed, spying her over Stu's shoulder. "There you are. . . . At least I think it's you behind those glasses. How can you see in here with those things on? I've been looking all over for you."

Brian watched in amazement as Tory's frozen expression turned to delight. "Carson! What are you doing here?" She hugged the stranger, who returned the embrace enthusiastically.

"Well, you wouldn't tell me when you were coming home, so I flew down to try to help you decide."

"What fun! And you couldn't have timed it better," Tory said gaily. "I've just finished my business here. How fast can you get your plane back in the air?"

"As soon as they finish putting in gas, I guess. But—"

"Wonderful! I'm ready to go. There will be fireworks at the club tonight, won't there?"

"Well, yes, but I thought you said—"

"It sounds fabulous!"

Tory was halfway out the door, pulling Carson in her wake, when Don spoke up, sounding confused. "Wait a minute. What about Mr. Harper . . . from San Francisco? He'll be here tomorrow to meet you."

"Thanks for reminding me," Tory said, pausing. "I'll just have to call him and reschedule for later in the week in Seattle. I'm sure whatever's left of this business can be accomplished then." She darted back to the desk and scooped up several of the glossy NorthPointe brochures that had been lying there. "Don't want to forget these. My friends will love them. Don, I'll be in touch. Nice meeting you, Mr. Merritt." Swiftly, she turned and strode out the door. Smiling apologetically at the others in the room, Carson followed her.

Astonished at her precipitous departure, Don and Stu looked at Brian. "She didn't even say good-bye to you, Brian," Don finally said. "I thought . . . I mean . . . I thought you two were . . . That's what Sarah said anyway."

"Well, Sarah was wrong," Brian said.

"Who's Carson?"

"Somebody who belongs to 'the club,' I guess."

Once outside, Tory deflected Carson's eager questions with a terse, "Please, not now. You've got a car? Let's get my things from the house." Carson led the way to a beige Buick Skylark parked nearby. Obviously, the rental company had finally located the car Tory was supposed to have had. She stiffened as she heard the door behind her open, then quickly stepped to the car and flashed Carson a brilliant smile. "I can hardly wait to get back to civilization and a real Fourth of July celebration," she announced without a backward glance. She wrenched open the door and dropped into the front seat.

Determined not to let herself think of the scene just concluded, she kept up a meaningless stream of chatter as she directed Carson to the house. Later, when she was alone, maybe she'd think about it, but not now, not while the ache in her throat grew steadily worse. She just wanted to collect her bags and get away from this horrible town. Carson was, of course, taking her animation all wrong, thinking she was exhilarated about seeing him, but she couldn't deal with that at the moment. One thing at a time.

"Tory, I'm so happy—"

"Turn right at the next corner."

"I mean, I didn't know how you'd feel about me showing up—"

"I was delighted to see you walk in, Carson. Really, I appreciate it."

He laughed. "I can see why. What a dumpy little town. This must have been the longest weekend of your life. A Saturday night here would be hard to imagine!"

Pointing, she said, "Up ahead there on the right, through the trees."

"You're kidding," he said as the house came into view. "That's it? That's your inheritance?" He slowed as he drove between the rows of trees and brought the car to a stop in front, staring just as Tory herself had done a few days ago. "Why, you ought to be able to sell that for . . . I don't even know how much . . . but mucho dinero. It looks like something out of a fairy tale. Wow! Does that make me the handsome prince, come to rescue you?"

Oh, shut up, she thought, unbuckling the seat belt with an impatient snap. Her temples had started to throb. "I'm long past the age of fairy tales, Carson. Too many princes turn out to be frogs."

Carson put a hand on her arm. "Not me, Tory. You know you can always count on me."

She looked at him, really stopped and looked at him for the first time since his arrival—and was instantly ashamed of the shabby way she was treating a friend. Her voice softened and her eyes at last filled with tears as she said, "Oh, Carson, of course I do. I'm so . . . so sorry—"

"Whoa. What's this? What'd I say?" he asked, gathering her into his arms.

At that, Tory cried harder. She cried for her stupid romantic ideas about Brian. She cried out of embarrassment at making a fool of herself, and out of remorse for using this wonderful friend to cover that embarrassment. After some time, the storm finally spent, she regained control and pushed him gently away. "Look, I'm not being fair to you at all. I'm glad to see you, really I am . . . but as a friend, Carson, just a friend."

"But back there you—"

"I know—that's what I meant about not being fair to you. It's a long story."

"That tall guy, right?"

"What?"

"Cowboy Bob back there in the office, the one you worked so hard to ignore?"

"Oh, Carson—"

"You're not going to start crying again, are you?" he asked, looking wary.

Her voice trembled. "If we don't get out of this town right now, I think I will."

"In that case, let's find your suitcase and get going."

"I wish I felt different about you, really I do."

"Are you sure, given a little time, that . . . ?"

"Very sure."

"Well, what can I say? If you ever change your mind, you know where to find me. You still want a ride back to Seattle?"

"I most certainly do."

"What about Cowboy Bob back there?"

"Cowboy Bob, as you put it, is one of those frogs I was just talking about."

Carson shook his head slowly. "Your weekend apparently wasn't as boring as I thought."

"Anything but," Tory said. "Oh, and there's one more thing. How do you feel about taking a dog back with us?"

"I thought you didn't like dogs."

"That was before I met this one."

He sighed. "This *has* been an eventful weekend. My plane is at your command, milady."

She kissed him on the cheek. "Carson, I don't think

I ever liked you better than I do right now. You're a terrific friend.''

''Thanks,'' he said glumly. ''That's just what I always wanted to hear you say. So where's this dog that's captured your heart?''

''He's usually right there on the porch,'' Tory said, getting out of the car at last. ''I can't imagine he's too far away.'' She walked around the side of the house, calling Jake and wondering if maybe Darla and Amy hadn't yet brought him home from the parade. Then she heard the sound of whimpering. ''Jake?'' She followed the sound until she could see his golden fur partially obscured behind the hydrangea bush by the kitchen door. ''Jake?'' she called again. He crawled toward her, but his face didn't look the way it had just an hour before. Now Jake looked as though he had suddenly sprouted enormous whiskers.

Carson halted behind her, looking apprehensive. ''What's the matter with him? Does he have rabies or something?''

Tory knelt beside the suffering animal and tried to comfort him. ''Not rabies. I think maybe he found a porcupine.''

''Why would he mess with a porcupine? What do we do now?''

''Poor Jake. Just relax, boy. We'll take care of you.''

''And just how are we going to do that? Do you know how to get those things out?''

Tory searched her mind furiously for an alternative to the obvious course of action, but she knew right away that the obvious solution was the only practical one available to them. ''No,'' she said reluctantly, ''but I know somebody who does.''

Chapter Eight

Jake was right behind Tory as she took the front steps two at a time and burst into the house. With shaking hands, she fumbled through the slim telephone book until she found the number of Don Thorne's office. The phone rang and rang in an empty room. "It's okay, boy, it's okay. We'll find Brian." She dialed again and breathed a sigh of relief when Brian answered at his clinic on the third ring.

"Brian?"

"Tory! Thank goodness . . . you don't know how—"

"Jake's full of porcupine quills. At least, I think that's what they are."

Suddenly, Brian was all business. "Can you manage him? Get him in the car?"

"I think so." She patted Jake, who now huddled against her leg. "He seems . . ." Her voice broke as Jake looked up at her, his muzzle bristling with sharp spikes. "He seems okay for now."

"Just hang on, Tory. Can you find your way to the clinic? Go back the way you first came into town, past the canal, on the road to High Desert. You'll see the clinic on the right—the low, white building. My truck's parked outside. Take you two minutes to get here."

Tory had no trouble persuading Jake to follow her back outside to the Mustang. He leaped into the passenger seat and settled beside her as though he'd been riding there for years.

"Shouldn't we lock up the house?" Carson asked, keeping well clear of the dog.

"No need for keys here, remember?"

"That was before I saw what a valuable place it is. You sure it'll be all right?"

"I'm sure. Just get in if you're coming!" Rather than disturb the dog, Carson clambered over the side of the car and fell into the backseat as Tory gunned the engine and shot off down the street.

Bracing himself as the Mustang careened around the corner, Carson muttered, "That place would be stripped clean in an hour in Seattle."

"Maybe so, but not here. Trust me. Anyone acting suspicious would stick out like a sore thumb, and Aunt Sarah could probably bust a crook single-handedly."

"*Aunt* Sarah?"

"Sarah Rafferty, Brian's Rafferty's aunt and my next-door neighbor. Brian's the vet we're taking Jake to see."

"But *Aunt* Sarah?"

Tory pulled up to the clinic in a spray of gravel and

jumped out of the car. "Never mind, Carson. I'll explain later."

Brian had left the front door open for them. As they ran into the empty reception area, he emerged from the back room, drying his hands on a towel. Tory remembered that the clinic was officially closed for the Fourth of July holiday.

"This way," he urged, leading them to the brightly lit examination room in the back. He knelt for a swift look at Jake, then gave a low whistle. "Easy, boy, easy," he said as he picked up the dog and gently set him on the high table. With sure hands, he pried Jake's muzzle open and looked inside his mouth. "Uh-oh. You got a real good bunch, didn't you? See, Tory?"

He moved aside so that Tory could look for herself. Her stomach turned over at the sight. Jake's tongue sprouted more of the same spikes that were so conspicuously displayed on his face. "Oh, Jake. What were you thinking?" she said.

"Don't imagine there was a whole lot of thought involved. He saw a porky and took off after it." Brian shrugged. "It happens. Never heard of Jake doing it before, though. With any luck, he won't try it again."

"It looks . . . it must be terribly painful."

"Yep. Those quills need to come out right away. I can get the ones out of his muzzle okay, but no way to get them out of his tongue, especially the back part, without putting him all the way out. He's a good dog, but not *that* good. Every one of those quills has to be cleared out or they'll fester—now and then they even work their way up through the roof of the mouth to the brain."

"And do what?" Carson moved closer and entered the conversation for the first time.

Brian frowned at him. "What do you think? Kill him."

Tory gave a little moan. "Then do it. Get them out now."

"Right. I'll get Cindy down here to help with the anesthetic. See he doesn't try to jump off the table." He went to the other room to call Cindy while Tory stroked Jake and whispered soothing words.

"That's the same guy," Carson said in a low tone.

"What?" Tory was only half listening.

"The guy from the office," he said, "the one you were so careful not to notice before. Cowboy Bob."

Tory leaned her head against Jake's warm shoulder. She felt fresh tears welling up. Her eyes still hurt from the earlier bout of weeping; her face felt hot and tight. She couldn't bear to explain all this to Carson, not right now. "Please, Carson, just let it alone."

"What's going on, Tory? You only met him . . . what . . . three, four days ago? What did he do?"

"Nothing . . . he didn't do anything. Just keep your voice down," she said desperately, "and please, please, don't ask any more questions."

"I've never seen you this way before," he announced, wonder in his tone. "You're in love with him."

"Don't be silly. I can't stand him. Now just—"

"Sure," Carson said, as Brian came back into the room. "I understand, Tory. I really do."

"Cindy's on the way. Shouldn't take her long."

Tory dashed the tears from her eyes and hoped that Brian would think her obvious distress was related to Jake's condition. An uncomfortable silence fell over the room, broken only by the sound of Jake panting as he tried to keep cool on this warm summer afternoon. Tory scrutinized the jars and instruments standing on the nearby counter with the concentration of someone taking an inventory: cotton swabs, long Q-Tips, a lighted device for looking into ears and eyes, a thermometer upright in an antiseptic solution, prescription pads.

Meanwhile, thoughts scurried around in her head. *Don't let him know. Don't let him know how he's hurt you. After all, he can't see what you're thinking, and you've never actually said anything about your feelings. Pretend he never interested you. Just get through the next few minutes. Concentrate on Jake.*

"What exactly is the procedure?" she asked, surprised that her voice sounded quite businesslike. "The complete treatment?"

"Pretty basic stuff. Put him all the way out and remove the quills. Easy enough as long as you're careful to get them all. Then he takes an antibiotic for a few days to head off any possible infection."

"And he'll be all right?"

"Don't worry. He'll be just fine."

"Good." Tory masked her relief with a brisk manner. "Then we can be out of here pretty much on schedule."

"Whoa. Not so fast. With this many quills, and a general anesthetic, I don't want him going anyplace, at least till tomorrow."

Tory twisted her hands together out of sight behind her back, pressing the thumbnail of her left hand into the flesh of her right palm in an attempt to focus on something other than Brian's face across the examining table. How could he stand there looking so earnest, so handsome, causing her heart to turn over even when she knew what a fraud he was? She needed to get out of here fast. "Nonsense. Couldn't we just carry him to the plane? Surely he'll be fine in a couple of hours."

"Could be, but he also could wake up vomiting and choking. Doesn't seem like a very bright move to risk him that way."

"Well," she said, defeated, "I guess since you put it that way, maybe he'd better stay overnight." She'd get Carson to pick him up in the morning. No matter what, she was not setting foot in this clinic again.

"Actually, I'd like to observe him for several days. It's important to make sure all the quills are out." Tory searched Brian's face for some hint that he was manipulating the situation to keep her here. She wouldn't put it past him to delay her departure so he could make an attempt to charm her into changing her mind about the house. At this point, she wouldn't put anything past him. His face gave away nothing, and she felt helpless in this situation. Unfortunately, she didn't know enough about dogs and porcupine quills to be able to determine whether he was making all this up.

As she hesitated, not wanting to risk hurting Jake just to spite Brian, suddenly her hurt and despair gave way to a fierce, primitive anger that boiled up from her very core. The arrogance of the man! He thought he was so smart. Well, he might have the upper hand in this situation, but she'd find some way to take him down a peg. She didn't know yet what she'd do, but before she left Silver Pine, she intended to hurt him the way he had hurt her.

Out of the blue, Carson came charging into the struggle, like some crazed knight from out of the fairy tale that Tory had been so recently constructing. He wasn't the knight she'd been hoping for, but his unexpected words cut through the problem like a very welcome lance.

"Tory . . . darling . . . maybe you can send for the dog in a week or so. Couldn't you board him here or something?" Carson put his arm protectively around Tory's shoulder and spoke to Brian. "I didn't want to spoil the surprise, but the party tonight at the club is in honor of our engagement—"

"Our . . . engagement?" Tory echoed faintly, giving a small start. Their engagement was certainly news to her, but even in her distress, her quick mind seized immediately on the possibilities in the deception. Her dear friend Carson, reading the situation between her and Brian clearly, was giving her an out. His act of kindness threatened to overwhelm the emotions she was trying so hard to keep in check. Why couldn't she love this wonderful man instead of wasting her tears on a charlatan like Brian?

"I was afraid you'd be unnecessarily delayed," Carson improvised gamely, "and that's why I . . . ah . . ."

Brian's shocked expression immediately spurred Tory to join in the charade. "Oh, Carson," she gushed. "How sweet of you. I had no idea." That part, at least, was true.

"Neither did I," Brian said in a low voice. After a small pause, he added, "Congratulations."

"Thanks," Carson said, giving Tory's shoulder a squeeze. "Now, how about it? Will that work all right? We really do need to get going . . . darling."

"I don't see why not," Brian said. "Of course, if taking care of Jake is too inconvenient for your busy lifestyle, you don't need to take him at all. I know Sarah'd be glad to keep him permanently." His unconcealed sarcasm fanned the flames of Tory's fury to a white-hot pitch. She hoped he would mistake the redness of her cheeks for excitement at her "engagement" party.

Offering a mental apology to Jake, she said lightly, "Maybe that *would* be best. Oh, I just can't think it through right now. This party, the surprise . . . well, it has me all up in the air. You should have told me before, Carson. I'd never have stayed away from home this long if I'd known about it." She took a perverse pleasure in seeing the bafflement in Brian's eyes. *Take that, you phony. If I can keep up this act for two more minutes, maybe you'll think I was just playing you along, instead of the other way around, as you planned.*

She bent to pet her dog one last time, turning away from Brian so he wouldn't see her torment. She thought, Jake, I promise to send for you as soon as you're well— but somehow I'll do it without having to deal with the smug Dr. Rafferty. Straightening up again, she manufactured a smile and said, "Okay, let's go, Carson."

Brian put a protective hand on Jake's back and struggled to control his rage. Of all the cold-blooded, callous acts he had ever seen, this was about the worst. He could hardly believe it, but Tory was going to walk out and leave her injured dog just like that, without so much as a backward glance. "Don't you even—"

"Got here fast as I could." Cindy came flying in the door, her precipitous entrance stopping Brian in mid-sentence. "Oh, poor Jake," she said, "don't you know that dogs don't win contests with porcupines?"

"Thanks for coming, Cindy," Brian said.

"Sure. Hi, Tory. Sorry to meet you again like this,

you know, but don't worry. Brian will fix Jake up good as new. In a couple days, he'll be his old self. Good thing he didn't do this earlier today. Course if he had, he could have gone as a porcupine in the parade.'' She giggled at her little joke, but soon stopped when no one else joined in.

Brian watched Tory dig around in her purse for something. No wonder she couldn't find whatever she was looking for, since she still wore those stupid dark glasses that made her look like some visiting rock star. She hadn't worn them before today, but then today was the day her mask had come off, the day she'd shown her true personality. What had she been doing this weekend? Slumming and killing time so she'd have amusing stories to tell back at ''the club''? She had certainly fooled him, though, pretending to be interested in him and Jake and Silver Pine—until her fiancé showed up, that is.

She stopped looking in her purse and said, ''Please continue. Don't I even what? Oh, yes, the bill. You probably want some money up front before you'd be willing to take care of the dog. Carson, would you be a darling? I don't think I have enough money on me—''

Carson's wallet was already in his hand. ''Sure, honey. How much do you need?''

''Forget it.'' Brian said.

''Oh, but I insist,'' Tory said. ''It's best to get things clear right up front, don't you think? That way there are no nasty surprises later.''

''I'm not after your money,'' Brian said deliberately.

Tory tossed one of her embossed business cards onto the examining table. ''Well, just send the bill to my office. We really don't have time to debate this now.''

Brian stood speechless with fury for a moment before

he comprehended that Tory was actually leaving. Could he really have been this wrong about her? On impulse, he caught her arm just as she reached the door and, in a voice pitched low so that no one else could hear, he tried one last time. "Tory, don't let your feelings about me spill over onto everything else—"

"I don't know what you're talking about. As you can plainly see, I have a fiancé, so I certainly don't have any 'feelings' about you, as you put it."

"You know what I mean . . . Jake, the sale . . ."

Tory's mouth worked curiously, and for a minute Brian thought she was about to smile. It was hard to tell anything about her expression when she was insulated behind those glasses, though.

She said at last, "You leave me no choice but to be brutally frank. Somehow you have received a very much mistaken idea. My decision to sell to California Development is strictly business . . . a wonderful opportunity . . . and it in no way concerns you." She shrugged off his hand as someone might brush away a fly. "As for the dog, I never asked for him and, when Carson and I get married, he won't fit into our plans at all. Now, if you'll excuse me, I have a plane to catch."

Chapter Nine

"Howdy, Carson, Tory!" Clint, the savvy doorman at Longhorns West, greeted them with all the counterfeit enthusiasm his job demanded, even though he had never met Tory before a moment ago. He raised his voice to make himself heard over the heavy bass beat of the country band laboring nearby. "Missed you folks this week. Mighty glad t' make yore acquaintance, ma'am." Tory just nodded, finding conversation all but impossible in this place. Clint continued, apparently used to the up-roar around him. "Heard you were in Oregon pickin' up tips on the *real* Wild West for us." He tipped his black Stetson further back on his carefully styled hair and hooked his thumbs into the front loops of his designer jeans. "Whadda ya think . . . Are we authentic or what? Hey, Carson. Roped 'er and brought 'er back to the ol' corral, I see."

Since the nightspot had just opened recently, Tory

doubted that he had too many deep-seated feelings about the desirability of her being roped and brought back to the ol' corral. How on earth had she let Carson talk her into coming to this place?

After their silent flight back to Seattle from Silver Pine, all she had wanted was to crawl off somewhere and be alone, but Carson had been so anxious to help once they'd landed that she had reluctantly agreed to come along for a while. "We've found a new place," he urged her. "Getting out with friends tonight will do you good, even if you don't want to go to the club for the fireworks." She'd finally let him persuade her. After all, she had to begin somewhere in getting on with her life after this disastrous trip, but if she'd known Carson had in mind an urban cowboy bar, she'd have waited until another day to make a fresh start. Longhorns West was the newest discovery of their crowd, and in that fast-moving group, mere acquaintances were pronounced friends as soon as possible. They were dropped with equal rapidity when the group moved on.

"Sorry, but I didn't see anyone in Silver Pine wearing anything remotely like your outfit," Tory said, eyeing Clint's yellow silk neckerchief, shiny shirt, and pointed snakeskin boots.

"You what?" Clint shouted. "Can't hear you."

"No snakeskin boots."

"What?"

Tory surrendered to the noise and gave him the thumbs-up sign as she shouted, "You look great, Clint-baby, like a real Oregon cowboy."

Clint nodded. "That's what I thought."

"There's Gina. C'mon." Carson took her elbow and together they plowed through the crowded dance floor toward a table on the other side. As they made their slow way under the flashing lights and between the sweating dancers, Tory felt assaulted by the congestion and the noise. Was it always this way here or was she merely contrasting it with the tranquillity of Silver Pine?

When they finally reached the table and sat down, the music crashed to a halt and the band members put down their instruments in preparation for a break. Maybe someone had paid them to stop, Tory thought. She certainly would have if it had occurred to her. Gina and Tory greeted each other with their customary mutual lack of enthusiasm. Gina was dressed all in black, as usual, and smoking a cigarillo. After hearing her first words, Tory found herself thinking that maybe the noise of the band would have been preferable to a conversation with Gina.

"Wasn't it fun the way Carson flew down to pick you up from . . . what was it . . . 'Possum Hollow'?" Gina darted a quick look to see whether Carson appreciated her little joke, but Carson was watching Tory.

"Silver Pine, Gina. I was in Silver Pine," Tory explained.

"Bet you were surprised to see him."

Now Tory smiled a real smile for the first time since entering Longhorns West a few minutes ago. Looking at Carson, she said, "Totally surprised—and very, very glad."

Marlys drifted up in a cloud of Obsession, looking bored as usual. "Glad about what?" Her fringed shirt and denim skirt were supposed to help Marlys fit into the ambiance of Longhorns West, but the designer labels ruined that down-home image she was trying to cultivate.

Gina said, "Glad Carson rescued her from that hick town in Oregon."

"Oh, yes," Marlys said. "When we heard you were stuck there for the whole weekend, we wondered whatever you'd find to do with yourself."

"Oh, I managed," Tory said.

"Doing what?"

"There was the house to check out, papers to sign . . . that kind of thing."

"The house was spectacular," Carson volunteered. "With a little fresh paint—and the serious attention of a housekeeping and gardening crew—it would fit right in on Queen Anne Hill, wouldn't it, Tory?"

"Really?" Marlys sounded a shade more interested. "Too bad it's sitting in the middle of a cactus field or whatever."

"No cactus, Marlys. There's a lot of sagebrush outside of town . . . and beautiful wildflowers, but the house itself is surrounded by old-growth ponderosa pines on one side and aspen lining the drive on the other. Wolf River is just out of sight through the pines." That picture would stay with her always, something to cherish.

"Whatever. Sounds primitive." Marlys was negative, as always.

Tory pulled back, stung. Obviously, she was boring them. The beauty of Silver Pine was too far outside their usual frame of reference for them to imagine, but then what could she expect from people who chose a place like Longhorns West to get their ideas about Western culture?

Ted, to whose arm Marlys clung like a bat, seconded her opinion. "No sports bar in town where you could catch the Mariners, I suppose."

"Not that I noticcd, but beautiful . . . and so peaceful."

"If you like looking at a bunch of trees," Gina said scornfully.

"Didn't Carson mention something about a parade?" Ted asked. "Some kind of animal thing?"

"A real Old West cattle drive? How quaint. I haven't heard about this," Gina said.

"Not a cattle drive. The pet parade. It's a local tradition . . . every year for forty-eight years they've had a pet parade on the Fourth of July," Tory said.

"Do tell. And here we were, afraid you wouldn't be able to find anything amusing to do," Gina said, laughing.

"Too bad you didn't have a pet to parade," Marlys drawled.

"Well, actually, I did. A dog."

"How'd you manage that? You don't own a dog." This from Ted.

"I do now, or I will in a week or so. A golden retriever named Jake. He sort of came with the house, and he was in the parade."

"Such excitement!" Gina offered. "I'm surprised you let Carson drag you away from all that thrilling activity. How could you bear to come back to tame old Seattle?"

And aren't you sorry I did, you sarcastic little fool? Tory thought.

"Wait a minute." Marlys said. "You can't keep a dog in your building. Remember when Annette and Unser got that little Shih Tzu? They were looking at an apartment in your building, but the regulations didn't allow dogs. By the way, have you seen that beast recently? Annette has him all decked out in matching bows on his ears and collar, but he has the most disgusting rash all over his body. They're taking him to a pet therapist— something about stress. Of course, living with Annette and Unser, I'm not surprised.''

Tory abruptly stood up, having listened to this idiotic conversation for as long as she could. ''Carson, I'm awfully tired. Could you run me home?''

''But it's early yet,'' Carson said. ''Are you sure?''

The band members had returned from their break and started tuning up again. ''Oh, yes. I'm very sure,'' Tory said.

For a long, weary moment, Tory's hand rested on the cold number pad in front of her, unable to remember the code she needed to press in order to allow access to her building. A far cry from the simplicity of the unlocked front door in Silver Pine. All her thoughts seemed to be moving in slow motion, and she looked without interest through the glass doors at the marble bank of elevators facing her across the lobby. At last the proper numbers came to her and she slowly punched them in. The door slid open with a well-oiled sigh, and she entered the lobby, stumbling a little. Carson caught hold of her arm.

''You really are tired, aren't you? But are you sure you don't want to come out with us for just a little longer? I hate to leave you alone like this. A little dancing and fireworks at the club maybe? Can't hurt . . . might even help.'' He smiled encouragingly.

''Thanks, Carson, but I've had about enough for one evening. I'm just not in the mood for any more loud places. You go along. Gina will be delighted to see you show up alone . . . and Ted and Marlys.'' She pushed the button and leaned against the wall to wait for the ele-

vators. Ted, Marlys, and Gina. They seemed to belong
to another lifetime—and she didn't want to talk to any
of them. Keeping up a bright, social conversation for any
longer than she already had tonight was way beyond her
ability right now.

The elevator's soft chime indicated its arrival and she
pulled herself upright from the wall. "No, Carson. Don't
come up. I'll be fine. I just . . . I'll be fine."

"Are you sure? How about lunch tomorrow? You can
try out Le Chat Sceptique yourself."

"Not tomorrow. I'll need to catch up with . . . whatever . . . at the office." She waved her arm vaguely, then
let it fall to her side. "Right now I can't think what all,
but I know there's plenty. Go on—have some fun." She
forced a smile to her face and continued, "After all, it's
the Fourth of July." Her voice broke.

"Tory," Carson said, moving toward her helplessly,
"you know I'd do anything—"

"I know—and you've already done plenty. . . ." Her
voice trailed off as the memory of that painful scene in
Brian's office returned in all its intensity. "I'll never
forget your kindness this afternoon."

"I should have punched that jerk!" Carson said.

"No, you shouldn't have." She didn't think it either
necessary or kind to mention that in any fistfight with
Brian, Carson would certainly come out on the short end.
Still, his heart was in the right place. "You were great."
The *pop-pop-pop* of fireworks exploding somewhere in
the distance brought her back to the present. "And now,
my favorite defender, it's time for you to go on to the
club . . . or wherever the group is headed next . . . and for
me to get some sleep. Thanks for everything." She

stepped into the elevator and blew Carson a kiss as the doors swished shut.

Even though Tory's professional cleaning service had been on duty during her absence this week and left everything in its usual precise order, Tory paused in the doorway and studied her penthouse living room with un-accustomed dislike. All neutral colors and slashes of bold abstracts on the wall, it could belong to any one of a dozen high-priced hotel rooms she had stayed in, and, in spite of the hard work of the air conditioner, the place retained the faintly musty smell of an uninhabited dwelling.

No friendly retriever welcomed her. Poor Jake. His day had been even worse than her own. Still, she felt sure that by now he was feeling better. Even though Brian might not be trustworthy as a man, Tory remem-bered his tender care for the cow on the road and knew that he would take excellent care of Jake. First thing in the morning, she'd start the wheels in motion to get him up to Seattle with her—even if she had to move to an-other apartment building to do it.

Her mail was piled neatly on the otherwise bare kitchen counter in the oppressively silent apartment. Without making a conscious decision to do so, she up-ended her purse and let its contents spill onto the sterile surface of the counter. Coins bounced and clattered to the floor, and a lipstick rolled right to the edge of the counter before she trapped it. There. Now it looked more as though a living, breathing person occupied this place. The only problem was that she had absolutely no idea what to do next in order to continue that illusion. She sighed as the silence returned.

Without looking, she knew that the stack of mail

would most likely contain some bills, numerous requests for charitable donations, maybe a flyer or two, and the latest copy of *Forbes*. Likewise, the refrigerator would be stocked with yogurt, juices, gourmet bagels—all healthful foods designed to be eaten on the run between appointments, not savored as a home-cooked meal served on fine bone china.

The red telephone message light blinked from the wall behind the counter. Probably a message from Marie, reminding her of her appointments for the next day. But, no, Marie wouldn't have known she was coming back tonight. Maybe . . . she pushed the button and listened, with a faint stir of hope, as a man's voice came on: "Ms. Baxter . . . ah . . . this is John Harper, attorney for California Development, hoping to catch you before you leave for Silver Pine. . . ." He went on to tell her how sorry he was about breaking their appointment and to give his telephone number, but Tory had lost interest.

The second message was a reminder of an upcoming committee meeting of the local hospital board. The third was a similar reminder about a benefit for the Youth Foundation. Next came notification that the alterations to her black suit at Nordstrom were finished. Finally, Marlys came on the line to tell her in some detail about how absolutely boring the housewarming party at the Hogans' new place on Lake Washington had been Saturday afternoon. She congratulated Tory on having missed it. Tory wondered, not for the first time, just how disappointed Marlys would be if she accidentally happened to like some activity, but decided that probably the situation would never occur. Holding her finger on the rewind button, she erased the messages. Nothing there of interest.

Feeling all at once too tired to cope, she slowly righted her bag and stuffed keys, lipstick, and wallet inside. Against the toaster where it had landed, the little carved bear stood upright, still smiling at her. At first startled to see it there, she remembered that she had put it in her bag before going to the pet parade. Just this morning. She had intended to show it to Brian, but that impulse seemed a long, long time ago. "What are you smiling about?" she asked.

Suddenly, like an echo, she heard in her memory the very same question, only this time, it was her father's voice asking her mother that question as he came in the door from work one evening when Tory had been about ten years old.

He had set down his briefcase and asked his wife, "What are you smiling about?"

"Look, Richard," she had said, holding something out to him. "Isn't this a lovely carving—"

"From Jim?" His harsh tone had made Tory pause on her way in from the dining room to greet him, knowing that something was wrong.

"Yes." Now her mother sounded wary, but more determined than usual. "Richard, just take a look at how delicate the branches are—"

"I don't care if he sculpted them out of gold bullion."

"He's trying to . . . Can't you just let it go?"

"No, and I'll thank you not to raise this topic again. Do you understand me? Get rid of that thing before I get back." A slam of the door and he was gone.

Tory had ventured out at last, creeping to her mother's side and huddling there. Her mother put a gentle arm around her. "What's wrong?" Tory asked. "Why was Father so angry?"

Her mother stroked her long auburn hair back from her face and spoke earnestly. ''I'm sorry you had to hear that, Tory, but it's nothing to do with you.''

''What's that you're holding?''

''Just a package delivered by mistake.'' Her mother looked sad as she put a small carved tree back into the box from which it had come.

''But it's so pretty . . . and the package has our name on it.''

''I know, but it was still a mistake.''

What had happened to that package? Tory wondered now. Perhaps her mother had gotten rid of it, as ordered, because Tory hadn't seen it since that evening so long ago. Still, it was clear that her mother hadn't wanted to discard it, so maybe she hadn't.

Playing a hunch, Tory strode to the bedroom she used as a home office and snapped on the light. There in the closet was a neatly packaged box of belongings from her father's den that she had never thoroughly explored after his death. She had glanced at it once, but the top layer contained his home business records, and she had put it aside, thinking she'd get to it another time. Those records were duplicates of papers he kept at the office, so there was no hurry. The maids who had packed up their apartment had given Tory her mother's sentimental papers separately, including Tory's childish watercolor portfolio.

Now she dragged her father's box out into the center of the room and opened it. Layers of papers, just as she had thought, evidence of the long hours he had worked on NFM business, even when he was supposed to be relaxing at home in the evening. Nothing but papers. No, wait . . . there it was. The small package she was seeking was tucked down in the corner of the box, the original wrapping still around it, and it was addressed to Mr. Richard Baxter. That was why the maids had put it in her father's box after his death. How angry he would have been to know that his wife hadn't followed his instructions. How angry her father had been at so much in the world.

She shook the box and the little wooden tableau inside tumbled out. A carved pine trees, its branches carefully delineated in a dark hardwood, stood on a solid base that had the suggestion of a flowing river in the foreground. The piece was obviously designed to stand on a mantel or a coffee table. Tory didn't have to see the characteristic JSB to know who had done the exquisite carving.

She set the little pine tree on top of the box and returned to the still-dark living room. Without turning on a light, she crossed swiftly to the bank of windows on the opposite side of the room and pulled open the elegant draperies. Seattle's skyline was obscured by the rain and clouds that had greeted them on their arrival earlier. Naturally. Marie had warned her on the phone this morning about the threatening weather, but she had been so immersed in the warm sunshine of Silver Pine that the rain and clouds of Seattle had seemed far away. Impatiently, she flipped the lock and threw open the glass door to her deck. The rain-soaked air rushed in to billow the draperies and to spatter the carpet with water, but Tory just stood there, uncaring.

At last she faced the thoughts she had been trying to shove away all afternoon. Over and over she replayed today's events in her mind, trying to make them come out another way. She couldn't do it. The guilty look on Brian's face earlier had signaled unmistakably that he had been hiding his city council membership from her. He must have thought her so stupid that she'd fall into line with his opposition to California Development and their NorthPointe project just because he knew she found him attractive.

Was she really that gullible? No, she decided, he had hidden his true nature well, and she wasn't the first woman to have been taken in by a handsome face coupled with a seemingly attentive manner. She had merely been naive and trusting, certainly not characteristics her business associates would normally identify with her. In the midst of her gloomy assessment of the situation, she found one ray of sunshine. Even while attracted to Brian's charming, intelligent manner, she had recognized and questioned his obvious aversion to California Development. She hadn't simply accepted at face value his charges about how unscrupulous they were. After all, they were a well-established company, and she had no reason to doubt their ethics. However, from her own personal experience, she knew that Brian Rafferty could give lessons in deceit to a professional con artist.

At length, she shivered as the cold wind touched her face, her cheeks now wet with both rain and tears. It was all too much to take in tonight—Brian's betrayal, the sale of her house, the feud between her father and her uncle. What did it matter, what did anything matter? From out over Puget Sound came the intermittent booms and flashes of the Fourth of July celebrations taking place around the area. Was it still the Fourth of July? This day seemed to have been going on for a long, long time. Tory went back inside and closed the sliding doors.

Chapter Ten

From the time that the staff of Northwest Financial Management entered their suite of offices on the twelfth floor of the Parker Building the next day, they had no doubt that their boss was back, and ready to tackle work with a vengeance. Tory arrived before any of them, outwardly composed and perfectly groomed as usual in a crisp red-and-white polka-dot coat dress, her face showing nothing of the sleepless night she had just endured. After requesting an espresso and giving orders that she would not accept any calls, she disappeared into her private office.

All morning she worked steadily to catch up with the weekend's accumulated work, transferring papers methodically from one side of her desk to the other with hardly a pause until Marie tapped at the door to her office shortly before noon and hovered there, obviously anxious to say something.

"Yes, Marie?" Tory turned from the spreadsheet she was studying, but kept her fingers poised over the computer keys to indicate that she was busy.

"I know you don't want to take any calls just now, but Carson Finley has phoned twice to ask about lunch and Mr. Harper from San Francisco has already called three times. I thought maybe—"

"Oh, yes, the sickly Mr. Harper. He could have saved me a lot of trouble if he'd taken better care of his health." Tory swiveled her chair and sat looking out the window, finally standing up to pace back and forth in silence for a few minutes. "Next time he calls, put him through. Let's see"—she flipped open the Day Runner on her desk and paged through it—"maybe a meeting sometime early next week?"

"I thought . . ." Marie paused tactfully.

"You thought what?"

"Well, it's just that last week you said you wanted this settled quickly . . . and your schedule is now open Friday morning. Remember, the Benedetti meeting was shifted to the end of the month?"

"That's right. You told me earlier." Tory made a notation in the book, then resumed her pacing.

Marie hesitated in the doorway, not knowing whether Ms. Baxter wanted her to stay or go, and unable to guess what she was thinking. Ms. Baxter had been acting odd ever since the trip to Oregon. First the surprise flip-flop about Marie being able to stay home when Jeremy was sick, and now her uncharacteristic forgetfulness about rescheduling an important meeting. Watching in surprised fascination as Ms. Baxter walked slowly around the office studying various pictures, Marie felt her curiosity grow.

"What do you think of this, Marie?" Tory asked, pointing to a nearby lithograph.

Marie had always found it a depressing mass of lines and squiggles. She stalled. "Didn't your father pick that out?"

Ms. Baxter pressed her. "Yes, yes, but what do you think of it?"

"Really, I'm not qualified to judge. It's rather a valuable piece, I believe."

"You're hedging, but never mind. I agree with you. It's hideous."

After a few minutes, since her boss appeared lost in thought and didn't seem to have anything more to add, Marie started to withdraw to her own office. She'd try to ask about Mr. Harper later.

Tory stopped her before she could close the door. "Could you find the number of that decorator . . . what's her name . . . the one who did such a beautiful job with the renovation of the historical society?"

"Janine Laidlaw of Laidlaw Interiors. Certainly I can get the number for you, but you do know that her work is very traditional, some would even say old-fashioned."

"Yes, I'm aware of that, but this office . . . and my penthouse . . . are starting to seem stale. They need . . . something. I'm not quite sure what, but she'll have some ideas. Please make an appointment. I'd like to get started on that right away."

"I'll call her today. What about Mr. Finley?"

"I'll get in touch with him later."

Marie waited, but when Ms. Baxter didn't say anything more, she finally prompted, "About that Friday opening. . . ." Again came that uncharacteristic blank look. "Do you want to schedule Mr. Harper into that time Friday morning, assuming he's available?"

Another long pause. Maybe Ms. Baxter was sick or something. Normally she didn't hesitate over even the biggest decisions, but this one seemed to be causing her some real turmoil. Instead of answering the question, though, she marched across the room and pointed to an abstract acrylic in shades of red. "How about this?"

"No," Marie said promptly, suppressing a shudder.

Her boss nodded, and said, "We should have had this conversation a long time ago." At last she returned to her desk and stood behind it, hands braced on the glass top. "Okay, let's do it—the redecorating and the meeting—and the sooner, the better. Why shouldn't we get started? Then maybe things can get back to normal around here." From the strained look on her face, Marie thought she might well have been a general declaring war, instead of someone setting up a simple business meeting and preparing to choose a few new pictures for the wall.

"Fine. I'll put Mr. Harper through when he calls again. Oh, and Ms. Baxter, thanks again for letting me go home yesterday. Jeremy was feeling much better and we set off sparklers on the patio, just as you suggested."

"I'm glad it worked out for you."

"You sort of inspired me on the phone, the way you described the Fourth of July in Silver Pine. The pet parade and everything? It sounded so old-fashioned and friendly."

"That stuff's mostly for kids, of course."

"Oh, of course. I didn't mean that you . . . I mean, you're not the type . . . well, I don't know exactly what I mean, except that I can't quite imagine you surrounded by farmers at a country pet parade.'' Marie gave a little laugh. ''I'll put Mr. Harper through the next time he calls.''

Tory's burst of energy lasted until shortly after two, at which time she took a long look at the completed papers piled neatly beside her and, instead of her usual sense of well-being, she thought, ''So what?'' In all the years she'd worked to get to this position at NFM, not once before had that thought occurred to her.

Face facts, she told herself. *Your work isn't enough all by itself—and Brian's betrayal is a reality you can't wish away. You've got to start over, start from scratch to figure out what you want out of life. Getting Jake is the one good result of this whole painful experience. You'll have to write to Sarah and ask her to send him. No, not Sarah. That would end up involving Brian again. Better to go through Don Thorne.* It might be silly to pay an attorney to make the arrangements to ship a dog to Seattle, but it was the best alternative she could come up with.

Her intercom buzzed. ''Yes?''

''Mr. Harper on line two.''

''Thanks, Marie. Uh . . . Marie, have you called the decorator yet?''

''Not yet.''

''Well, better hold off a bit, just until I can check my building's policy about pets. I may have to move.''

''But you don't have a pet.''

''By next week, I will. Now put Mr. Harper on, please.''

Chapter Eleven

John Harper had fully recovered from his earlier, unexpected illness by the time he arrived at Tory's suite
of offices Friday morning to conclude the sale of her
property to California Development. From his tasseled
loafers and Armani suit to his blow-dried hair, he looked
every inch the successful corporate lawyer. His step was
brisk, his smile dazzling. Tory could guess that he
played racquetball three times a week at an expensive
health club, drove a dark blue BMW, and appeared reg-
ularly with a variety of stunning women at hot nightspots
around San Francisco. He'd probably love Longhorns
West.

Come on, Tory told herself, *what's your problem? The
guy's too well groomed? Maybe you'd prefer a man with
dark tousled hair and dusty jeans . . . a down-to-earth
guy who'd laugh uproariously at the idea of having his
hair styled? Don't forget that that same apparently*

down-to-earth guy is the one who deceived you, while this man standing in front of you hasn't done anything to make you mistrust him. He looks and acts just like every other successful guy you've ever dated. He comes from your world, for Pete's sake. What's the matter with that all of a sudden?

To make up for her unreasonable aversion to Mr. Harper, Tory greeted him with more warmth than was strictly necessary, putting them on a first-name basis right away. Unfortunately, he seemed to take this as an indication that the business meeting might turn into something more interesting later, and he turned up his charm accordingly.

As they settled into the comfortable leather chairs in the boardroom, he smoothed his expensive tie and admired the view of Puget Sound. "Now this is really something! I'm sorry you had to make an unnecessary trip last week, but I don't mind telling you that I'd rather spend the day in Seattle than Silver Pine. Not that I'd mind meeting you anywhere," he said gallantly. "Maybe you'll even consent to show a lonely out-of-towner something of your fair city later."

"Possibly," Tory murmured noncommittally. She wished he'd quit smoothing his tie, calling attention to it. She couldn't get the image out of her head of a future that included a series of predictable dates with men who all looked alike, sounded alike, and wore the same trendy ties.

He looked earnestly at her and continued. "Seriously, I hope you'll accept my apology for the inconvenience I caused you, Tory. California Development and I would like to make it up to you. You ski, of course?"

"Well, yes—"

"Then we'd like you to accept a week on us at NorthPointe Resort, good anytime you want to use it—after it's built, of course. The summer facilities ought to be available in about a year, but the ski lifts aren't projected to be operational for eighteen months. Right about time for a winter vacation, if everything goes according to schedule, that is."

"That's very good of you, John, but I assure you, my trip to Silver Pine was really no problem. I probably needed to see the place at least once, if only to understand the situation there."

"No, no, we insist. It's the least we can do to make up for the trouble my illness caused you."

"Well then, since you put it that way, I accept. That will be wonderful. But your time line . . . isn't that rather ambitious, to build an entire resort that fast?"

"That's right. It certainly is, but this project has a very high priority." He snapped open his Coach briefcase to reveal the neatly packed papers that would at last transfer ownership of Tory's Silver Pine house and property to the California Development Corporation. "I see you've been studying our brochures," he said, gesturing at the bright folders Tory had placed on the table before them. "You can see that this is going to be a big operation—I mean a really big operation—and the sooner we get started, the sooner everyone involved will be making a lot of money. I'm sure you don't have any objection to that.

"So, do you have questions, Tory? That's what I'm here for, though the faster we conclude these formalities, the sooner we can get to . . . other things." He leaned closer. If anything, his smile became wider. Tory was sure he normally did especially well with women clients, but she wished he'd stop smoothing that tie.

She sat back in her chair, gathering her thoughts. "Yes, I do have a few questions. But before we start, would you care for something to drink?" She pressed a buzzer on the underside of the table and soon they were sipping iced fruit juice out of frosted goblets.

Now that the actual sale was at hand, Tory found herself strangely reluctant to begin the final stage of this process, though there was certainly no point in waiting any longer. All she had left to do was to assure herself that California Development's project would not have the disastrous negative impact on the Silver Pine community that Brian had predicted. She was well aware that there was a good chance Brian had misrepresented their plans for her property, as he had so cunningly misrepresented his interest in her. Once she felt sure that she wouldn't be actually harming the small town by her actions, she could complete the sale and sever her ties with the place once and for all.

"Tell me a bit more about NorthPointe, John, and how it ties in with your plans for my house. I know that the resort site is located miles from town, so why put a sales office so far away from the project? There have been some rumors that your company is planning to spread its development in the direction of town, but, frankly, I wouldn't want to be a part of anything that changes the character of Silver Pine. On the other hand, I am pleased to see someone interested in investing money in the restoration of my house." Tory could see that John was listening intently as she spoke, and she found it reassuring that he was giving the matter his full attention.

"Those are excellent questions, Tory, and I believe that I can answer all your concerns. Let me say first that California Development has absolutely no interest in moving closer to Silver Pine. NorthPointe Resort will be out at Lodestar Peak or beyond—and any expansion will be away from town, not toward it. You don't need to fear that the little town will be impacted." He gave a small chuckle and joked, "Unless the townsfolk want to go skiing at NorthPointe or invest in the project—both very good ideas, I might add. Look, I'm not an engineer or anything, but you can see for yourself from the brochures that everything at this resort is being done right. No expense spared." He spread out one of the colorful pamphlets and pointed to various pages as he spoke. "World-class skiing, a lodge that will rival anything at Aspen, hiking, horseback riding, several golf courses." He leaned back and smoothed his tie again. "Just about anything you want for the vacation of your dreams. Frankly, you'd be amazed at the projections of growth in the area over a ten-year program. That sleepy little area will wake up fast!"

"That sounds like a major change," Tory said doubtfully.

"But it has nothing to do with Silver Pine itself, I assure you. If the prospect of Silver Pine changing presents a problem for you, just put it right out of your mind. California Development always strives to be a good neighbor. Don't let me mislead you, though. There's no doubt that NorthPointe Resort will be a real economic bonanza for people wise enough to see the possibilities. Once we get the condo sales rolling, people will be fighting to buy into the project.

"To be honest, Tory, that's where your house comes

in. I've only seen pictures of it, but our people say it's the most imposing structure in town. Puts the rest of the houses to shame. As I just told you, this project has the highest priority, so it's just plain good business to use a house that's already there for an office. After all, there are no telephone lines out at NorthPointe yet. Your house will be the starting point for the whole sales campaign. With just a little revamping, it'll make a terrific base of operations.''

''What do you consider 'a little revamping'? I really have come to love that old place, but since I don't intend to live in Silver Pine, it makes sense to put it in the hands of someone who will keep it up—paint it and take care of the grounds, for example.'' She realized how wistful she sounded and wondered fleetingly which one of them she was trying to convince of the wisdom of this course of action.

''Certainly—just a few cosmetic changes. They'll paint it, spruce it up in general. And they'll need extra phone lines, of course.''

''How about signs, parking?''

''Sure. A little sign, something tasteful . . . and parking for a few cars. Like I said, just a little revamping, nothing you'd really noticc.''

''That sounds all right, I guess,'' she said slowly.

''Good!'' He pulled the papers from his briefcase and tapped them on the table. ''Then shall we get started?''

''One more thing. There's been some local opposition, I understand, to your plans.''

''Oh, that.'' His smile faltered for a moment, then returned full force. ''You're a businesswoman, Tory, so you understand how things work. Some people just seem to be unable to appreciate any kind of progress.'' He shrugged. "Cranks . . . Every community has a few of them."

"I suppose. So you've faced this kind of difficulty before . . . with other projects? Zoning concerns and so forth?" Tory remembered what Brian had told her about the SouthPointe Resort project near San Francisco, of trees being cut before permits had been acquired, scars on the landscape that decades wouldn't remove. But perhaps that had just been Brian's propaganda.

"Nothing we haven't been able to handle. Most people like making money instead of making trouble." He looked pleased with his turn of phrase, and Tory knew he'd probably store it and use it again when making his next sales pitch.

"You've heard of the High Desert Land Trust?"

"Oh, that bunch," he said dismissively. "They talk a lot, like to make waves, but they don't have the capital to do much right now. By the time they get around to raising the kind of money needed to make an impact on the development nearby, we'll all have long, gray beards. Not you, of course," he joked.

"Nearby? But you just said all development would be miles away from Silver Pine."

"Oh, yes, of course. My error. I meant the development near NorthPointe."

"And my house will just serve as a contact point?"

"Absolutely."

"With just a few small changes."

He held up his right hand and spoke solemnly. "Believe me, Tory. You don't have a thing to worry about."

"I know it sounds silly, but I'd hate to see that house turned into something . . . tacky, or ugly."

"Yes, I understand perfectly. From the picture alone,

I can see why you'd feel that way. It's truly a beautiful old place.'' He pushed back his snowy white shirt cuff and looked at the Rolex on his wrist. ''Well, would you look at that. It's already past noon. If that about wraps up your questions, maybe we can get the boring paperwork out of the way and then have lunch together.''

The last thing in the world she wanted was to go to lunch with John, but what was the alternative? Another carton of yogurt at her desk? John was presentable, he was interested in having lunch with her, and he was not Brian Rafferty. That was the clincher. ''Yes, let's. I'm being much too sentimental about all this, and wasting your time in the bargain.''

He briskly swept aside the colorful brochures and placed in front of her a set of sterile typed sheets, yellow plastic tabs sticking out at the sides of some of the pages to mark the places at which signatures would be needed. ''You said your secretary would act as our notary?''

Tory sat, mesmerized by the contrast between the vivid hues of the sales brochures and the whiteness of the legal papers. Those stark, unadorned pages seemed so final. She wasn't sure she really wanted to do this, but, being realistic, she knew that some change was inevitable in the Silver Pine area, even if it were limited to the NorthPointe Resort up in the mountains. With or without her signature on those papers, California Development would set up an office somewhere in the vicinity of town. At least this way she'd know that her house would be cared for. She wouldn't ever go back there anyway, not as long as Brian lived in Silver Pine. Best to get the sale over with now and make a clean break.

''Tory . . . your secretary?'' John repeated.

''What? Oh, yes.'' Tory pressed the hidden buzzer,

and soon Marie appeared in the doorway. "Marie, we're ready for you now."

Marie hesitated as her telephone rang in the other room. "Let Stacy get that," Tory said. "Let's get this finished up."

Now that Tory had made her decision, she was anxious to get this sale over with. A moment later she scowled as Stacy tapped on the door and then poked her blond head into the room.

"Sorry to interrupt, Ms. Baxter, but there's a call—"

"Please, Stacy, no calls until we're through here."

"Okay, sorry." Stacy drew the heavy door closed behind her.

"You'll have to excuse Stacy. She's rather new and things have piled up since I've been away. Now, where were we?"

"No problem," John said easily. "It certainly saved time that you were able to have your attorney look these over this morning. Just a few quick signatures and we'll be having a quiet lunch at . . . wherever you think best . . . before—"

Another timid tap on the door brought a sharp, "Yes?" from Tory. Again, Stacy edged around the door frame, looking apprehensive.

"I'm sorry, but there's a call—"

"Hold all calls, Stacy." Tory spoke sharply. She had never before had this kind of difficulty with Stacy, usually a very intelligent young employee.

"Yes, but—"

"But what?" Tory rose from the table and strode toward the door, her annoyance plain from her tone.

Stacy gestured for Tory to come closer, then spoke in a low voice. "She said it was an emergency!"

"Who? What kind of emergency?" Tory lowered her own voice to match Stacy's, at the same time throwing a quick smile over her shoulder to reassure John.

"I don't know . . . some woman. She was very upset and hard to understand . . . something about ribbons on trees and a dog and . . . and I know this sounds crazy, but I think she said something about a rosemary bush. I'm sorry to bother you, but I didn't know whether to call the police or what." Stacy appeared near tears.

"That's okay, Stacy. I know who it is. You did the right thing." She thought for a moment and then sighed. "I'd better take the call. Switch it through to my private office, please." She returned to the conference table, shaking her head.

"Anything wrong?" John asked, rising to his feet.

"No, not at all, just a call I need to take right away. It won't take long."

"If it will help," he offered, "we could get these papers finished up first. Shall we do that?"

"That's kind of you, but really . . . this'll only take a minute. Marie, please get Mr. Harper another glass of juice if he'd like one and I'll be right back."

After closing the door firmly behind her and crossing to her desk in the next office, Tory sat in her chair and took a deep breath, preparing herself. Then she picked up the telephone. "Sarah? What's wrong?"

"Oh, Tory! Thank goodness you're there! It's Jake. I just didn't know what to do. Brian's over at Saunders Crossing . . . and Jake's . . . I don't know how to describe it—"

Fear gripped Tory. "Is he all right?"

"Well, yes, I guess . . . it's just that he was over at

your house again . . . you know how he keeps showing up there—''

''Yes, I know.''

''—only today was different. He wasn't around earlier, but didn't think a thing about it. He's been missing you something fierce all week, sort of moping around, I guess you'd say, and going over to your place a lot. Don't worry though . . . he's just fine now that he doesn't look like a pincushion anymore.''

Tory cut through the barrage of words. ''So what happened today, Sarah?''

''That's what I'm trying to tell you. After a while I heard him barking over there. He never barks—you know that—I don't think I've ever heard him bark, but he was just barking and barking.''

''And?''

''And I was right in the middle of putting up some raspberry jam, but he sounded kind of desperate, so I thought maybe he'd tangled with another porcupine—''

''Oh, no.''

''—so I just turned off the stove and went right over there.''

''And you found . . . ?'' Tory could have screamed with frustration. Was Jake all right or wasn't he?

''You know I don't meddle . . . but I didn't know what to do—''

''Please, just tell me what's going on.''

''That's what I was going to ask you, but I didn't want to meddle. I promised myself never again after the mess I made of things when I made Brian promise not to tell you about . . . and then you left all of a sudden . . . but of course no one here had the faintest idea that you were already engaged to that other young man—and I did so hope that you and Brian would . . . well, that's water over the dam.''

"Sarah!" Tory all but shouted into the receiver. "What's going on at my house?"

"I don't know. That's what I've been telling you. Jake's over there standing on the porch barking at all those men and he won't come to me at all. I've never seen him like this.''

"All what men?" Tory asked, dread starting to build within her.

"The men with the backhoe and a bulldozer . . . they're over stomping around in Ellen's herb garden. That's probably what set Jake off, seeing those big machines . . . but there's a couple more trucks there—a swarm of people putting ribbons on trees and taking pictures of the house and I don't know what all. So, if you don't mind my asking—''

"Blue plastic ribbons?" Tory asked faintly, remembering Brian's description of the ribbons appearing on trees that were about to be cut down—before anyone had gained proper permission to do so.

"How'd you know that?"

"Which trees?" Tory asked, knowing instinctively the answer she would receive.

"The big ponderosas between the house and the river. What's going on there? And what should I do about Jake?''

Tory's mind was racing now, fitting all the pieces together, and the more they fit, the angrier she became. California Development couldn't even wait for her signature on the final papers before starting work on their latest high-priority project. And she had almost fallen for it. The very idea of cutting down those trees—and a backhoe in Ellen's herb garden? What other "cosmetic changes" did they have planned?

" 'Cosmetic changes,' eh? We'll just see about that!"

"See about what? I don't understand."

"That's okay, Sarah. I do." Tory thought hard for a minute. "Is that deputy . . . Mike . . . oh, what's his name?"

"Mike Bonner?"

"That's the one. Do you know if he's anywhere around town today?" Even in the midst of her agitation, she knew what a silly question that was. If Mike was anywhere in Howard County, Sarah'd know his whereabouts.

"I saw him at the Shack having a double cheeseburger and fries a while ago."

"Could you . . . would you find him and ask him to call me at this number right away?"

"Sure, I can do that. But what about Jake?"

"Don't do anything about him. Once I talk to Mike Bonner, things ought to calm down pretty quick. Those men—and their machines and their blue plastic tape—should be off my property within fifteen minutes."

"Then it's still your property? You haven't sold it yet?"

"No, I haven't sold it, and I wouldn't sell to those . . . those buzzards at any price!"

"I still don't understand. What are they doing over there?"

"What they're doing . . . is leaving . . . whether they know it or not!"

"Should I go over and stay with Jake after I find Mike?"

"That'd be great, if you wouldn't mind."

"Mind? I can hardly wait to watch the show. Why, one of those men was downright rude when I tried to tell him he was stepping on Ellen's rosemary bush. I'll be glad to be shut of him. Don't worry, though, it's hard to kill a rosemary plant. Tory, you're . . . you're not mad at me, are you?"

"For calling? Oh, Sarah, you'll never know how glad I am that you did."

After giving Stacy instructions to put Mike Bonner's call through immediately, Tory remained in her office, thinking. Within five minutes, her private line buzzed and she gave Mike brief, highly specific instructions.

Next, she took a deep breath, arranged a smile on her face, and returned to the conference room. The now-restless John Harper turned from where he had been looking out the window. Something in Tory's expression must have alerted him to a change, for he reopened the conversation before she could do more than apologize politely for keeping him waiting.

"I know what you're going to say," he began.

"You do?" Tory asked in some surprise.

"You're going to live up to your reputation for toughness—now don't pretend that you don't have one—and hold up the sale until we discuss terms further."

"Really? Is that what I'm going to do?"

"That little charade about the telephone call. Come on now, we both know that there was no call—"

"Quite the contrary, I assure you. There most certainly was a call—two of them, as a matter of fact."

He looked at her admiringly. "You're a cool one, I'll say that. You seem so agreeable and yet . . . those papers aren't signed yet."

"No, they aren't," Tory agreed pleasantly. "Shall we sit down and discuss them some more?"

"I'd prefer it if you were to sit down and sign them," he said with a nervous laugh.

"Well . . ." she began, "I'm afraid that—"

"Why don't we cut to the chase? How much more do you want?"

"It really isn't a matter of money."

"Oh, come now. Please don't insult me, Tory. It's always a matter of money. The only question is how much?"

"I'm curious, John. Just how much are you authorized to offer?" she asked, watching with interest as beads of sweat appeared on his forehead, in spite of the room's superb air-conditioning.

"Just give me a number," he said.

"I've thought of a few additional questions. First, have you worked for California Development long?"

"Ten years. If that's what's worrying you, I can assure you that I have full discretion to negotiate more favorable terms on this deal."

"That's very reassuring." She smiled warmly at him. "Then possibly you worked on the SouthPointe project near San Francisco?"

"Well, yes, I certainly did. That was one of my biggest projects—and one of our most successful, I might add."

"Did you actually go on-site . . . visit the project from time to time?"

"Yes, that was part of my job."

"And what did you think of it?"

"What did I think of it?" He looked blank.

"Yes, how did you feel about the way the project evolved?"

"Why, I thought it was wonderful, of course. You'd hardly know the place now. Before, it was just a bunch of . . . well, nothing . . . and now, well, it's a fabulous resort area. Ah, I see where you're headed. You want in on the ground floor of NorthPointe itself. A very wise move. What would you like? Option to buy a condo? Favorable interest terms? Lifetime golf membership? You name it and I'm sure we can meet your terms. You're thinking that NorthPointe is going to make a lot of people rich, and you might as well be one of them."

"I do believe that you're right. A lot of people stand to make very big money on this project. Just for the record, could you tell me one more time, John, the exact plans your company has in mind for my house?"

"Of course, but we already went through all that. Your house will be the sales office for the project."

"And that project will be located entirely up in the mountains, not down near the town?"

"Well, more or less."

"Oh, more or less. That wasn't quite the answer you gave a few minutes ago. So you weren't being quite truthful when you said that no development was planned near the town itself."

"Well, I suppose it's possible that some future expansion might come in the direction of town, eventually." John's expensive necktie seemed to be fitting him a bit less comfortably than it had a few minutes ago.

"I don't suppose that you want the house as a starting point along the river for remaking the entire town as part of your expansion plans." When John didn't answer,

Tory pressed on. "And what will the house look like after you're through with your 'cosmetic changes'?"

"The exterior of the house will be preserved."

"But the inside will change?"

"Well, of course a few adaptations will have to be made to accommodate large-group presentations."

"Oh, large groups, of course. You forgot to mention that before. And the grounds?"

"What about them?"

"Blue plastic tape on trees? Does that mean anything to you?"

"The fools! They weren't supposed to—" He contained his sudden flare of anger quickly and attempted a return to his former easy manner. "That's nothing much. A couple trees will have to be removed—"

"Oh, yes, you mentioned needing space to park a few cars."

"Maybe a bit more than that," he said weakly. "Look, what does it matter? You won't own it anymore. Just tell me how much money you want."

"It matters to me. What exactly do you plan to park in the space where the trees presently stand?"

John was sullen in defeat. "Minivans for shuttling prospective clients up to NorthPointe after they see the presentations at the house."

"How many minivans?"

"Oh, I don't know—"

"Guess."

"Twenty to thirty, plus or minus."

"I see. Twenty to thirty. More than a couple trees would have to come down to make room."

"Maybe."

"And is that riverfront property zoned to allow all this commercial activity within the city limits?"

"That's not a problem."

"Probably not—as long as you have three of the five Silver Pine City Council members convinced that their town is about to become the next Lake Tahoe. I understand your need for haste. Gil Corcoran leaves this fall—there's your third vote—and by then the other city council members and the High Desert Land Trust people opposed to you might be able to gather enough muscle to slow things down."

John Harper didn't look dapper anymore. He merely looked worn out. "You should have been an attorney, but I wouldn't want to be on the opposite side of a trial from you. Okay, you know what's at stake, and you want your fair share. What kind of deal do you require so we can wrap up this sale here and now?"

"No deal and no sale."

"NorthPointe is going to open up and you're going to miss out—"

"Then I'll miss out."

"That's not good business, and it won't stop us. NorthPointe goes forward, with or without the sale of your house."

"Probably so, but this is the one part of your rotten scheme I *can* control." Tory stood up, eyes blazing. "You're not ripping up my house to make it into a large-group presentation hall, and you're not cutting down my hundred-year-old ponderosas!"

"Name a figure!" John stood too and held out his hand imploringly.

Tory ignored it. "And you're not ruining my aunt's rosemary plant. I think, under the circumstances, that we'd better skip lunch, don't you? Have a pleasant flight back to San Francisco, John. When you fly over SouthPointe going home, take another look. I've heard it's easy to spot from the air—the scars go on for miles.''

''You have no idea what kind of money you're losing out on. Look, I'll call you again next week—after you've had a chance to think it over. You'll be sorry—''

''Don't bother. I've been sorry about a few things in my life so far, but I guarantee that this isn't going to be one of them.''

Chapter Twelve

The following Monday morning, Tory found herself fidgeting through her quarterly meeting with C. J. Sheffield, who was usually her favorite client. Though she customarily looked forward to seeing him and enjoyed listening to his offbeat financial ideas for his investments, somehow today she was having trouble concentrating on the changes he wanted made to his portfolio. While C. J. talked, she took notes, but after a while she started sketching the head of a long-eared dog along the border of the page, filling in the background with a suggestion of pine trees. Eventually, she became aware of a prolonged silence in the room and looked up, startled, to find C. J. regarding her quizzically.

"Is something the matter, Tory?"

"What? No, of course not."

"Then from your notes, am I to surmise that my portfolio will soon include trees and a dog?'' He gestured at her drawing.

She blushed crimson and stammered, ''I'm sorry . . . you see . . . well, I *was* listening—''

''I'm sure you were. I'm only teasing.''

His gentle smile encouraged her to disregard her self-imposed rule about keeping personal matters out of the office. ''The truth is that my dog is supposed to arrive from Oregon by plane this morning . . . and I'm wondering why someone from the airport hasn't called yet.''

''Funny, I never figured you to be a woman who'd have a dog. Dogs mess up the rugs, need to be walked and taken to the vet, tie you down. They're a lot of work for a busy person.''

''That's what I used to think too, before I met Jake. He's a great dog, a golden retriever—''

He held up his hand. ''Say no more. I understand. Wouldn't have any other kind. Tasha goes everywhere with us—she was on the sailboat this past weekend, you know. She goes to the beach, in the car, everywhere. Dogs can really get to you, can't they?''

''They certainly can. You *do* understand.''

''So, with that in mind, would you like to take a break now and check with your secretary to see whether Jake has arrived?''

''Thanks, if you don't mind.'' She pressed the buzzer under the conference room table, bringing Stacy to the door. ''Has anyone from the airport called yet?''

''No, they haven't, Ms. Baxter.'' Stacy was all smiles today.

Tory wondered what that was all about. Stacy must have had a good weekend, or at least a better one than Tory had put in. After that one satisfying moment Friday when she had sent John Harper on his way, it had been a bleak several days. She'd tried and tried to come up with a reasonable excuse to justify getting in touch with Brian to tell him that her engagement to Carson was just a hoax—but she'd backed away from the idea every time. If she tried to explain the situation, she'd only sound ridiculous, and besides, even though Brian's distrust of California Development had proved right, Tory couldn't forget that he hadn't been honest with her.

But during that incoherent telephone conversation Friday, Sarah had said something about having extracted a promise from Brian. In the midst of the chaos of that day, Tory hadn't been exactly sure what Sarah had been talking about, but over the weekend, she had found herself tossing and turning for hours each night, trying to figure it out, unable to get the flickering hope out of her mind that maybe Brian had had a good reason for concealing his city council membership. Maybe he hadn't been pretending an interest in her simply to slow down the NorthPointe project. But if that were true, if he were interested in her, why hadn't he contacted her since? Because she had stupidly told him she was going to marry Carson, that was why. Around and around her thoughts had gone all weekend, always returning to the same hopeless place.

The prospect of Jake's arrival was the one bright spot she could see ahead of her—and now where was he? "Well, thank you, Stacy. Please let me know immediately when they call. And be sure to tell Marie the same thing."

"Will do," Stacy answered, laughing as she left.

"Your secretary is certainly in a good mood today," C. J. commented.

"Yes, she is," Tory responded. "I don't know what's gotten into her."

"Nice to see someone that cheerful."

"If you want to see 'cheerful,' you ought to meet Cindy."

"Cindy?"

"Someone I met last week on a trip to Oregon. Cindy takes the all-time prize in the good-humor department."

C. J. looked thoughtful. "You know, Tory, I may be way out of line to mention this, but I've known you since you were a little girl, so I'll do it. Call it fatherly advice from an old friend of the family, if you want. I'm very glad to hear that you have a dog. You've always seemed so very . . . serious for someone your age. Of course, I'm delighted that you're serious in the way you go about investing my money, but I've always thought you could use a little more—shall we say—frivolity in your life. After all, you're a beautiful, intelligent young woman, and I can't believe that having a hefty bank balance is the pinnacle of your dreams right now. I know that your father couldn't imagine anything more interesting than the workings of this office, but that was Richard, and he was certainly one of a kind." He shook his head at the memory before returning to his previous thought. "But there *are* other things in life . . . someone to love, a sailboat maybe, a good dog. . . . In the long run, things like that will make a person richer by far than any financial deal, no matter how lucrative. I like making money, but that's not the whole story." He stopped, embarrassed by the intensity of his words. "Okay, end of speech," he said briskly, but when he looked at Tory, he saw that he had apparently struck a responsive chord. Her eyes glistened with tears.

" 'Richer by far...' I was thinking the same thing about my aunt and uncle recently," Tory said in a low voice. "Thanks, C. J. I've always thought you were a smart man. Now I know you're a very smart man." She drew in a deep breath and turned to a fresh page in her notes. "Well, since Jake hasn't arrived yet, shall we continue making money for you?"

By the time Tory finally made her way back to her private office half an hour later, her vague disquiet about Jake was becoming a definite concern. Still no telephone call about his arrival. He should have been here long before this.

Upon opening the door, she immediately detected the pungent fragrance of pine. Resting incongruously on her otherwise bare, glass-topped desk was a large bough of ponderosa pine. She slowly approached it, heart hammering, but found no card, nothing by way of explanation. Sinking into her large leather chair, she allowed herself to absorb the distinctive aroma for a long moment before pressing the buzzer for Marie.

"Yes, Ms. Baxter?" came the familiar voice, her usual efficient manner tinged with uncertainty.

"Do you... could you tell me...?" Tory stopped, afraid to ask the question.

"Oh, Ms. Baxter," Marie said, "I hope that's all right ... I mean ... that I let him put that, that—whatever it is—fir bough on your desk—"

"Pine," Tory corrected, as she began to hope. "Ponderosa pine. You can tell by the number of needles—"

"He said, he said—"

The door opened and suddenly Brian filled the space where it had been. He was dressed for the city in a tweed sport coat, white shirt open at the throat, well-pressed jeans, and cowboy boots. "Don't blame Marie," he said. "I told her that pine was the Oregon version of an olive branch."

"It is? I mean, you did?" Tory stood up, but her legs felt weak and she leaned against the desk. "Brian—"

"Brought you something else from Oregon too," he said. A golden blur rushed by him and hurtled across the room to Tory.

"Oh, Jake, I've missed you!" Tory buried her head in the dog's soft fur. "You're all right now. No more quills." Jake's wild gyrations seemed to indicate complete health and satisfaction with everything around him. "But . . . but what's he doing up here in this office? Dogs aren't allowed in the building."

"That's what the fellow downstairs tried to tell us," Brian replied, "but it turns out he was wrong." As he spoke, he advanced across the room with long-legged strides. "Jake came all this way to see you . . . and I thought he might need some care on the plane, so I tagged along." Deliberately, he circled the desk until he was standing directly in front of her. "One or two things we need to talk about, near as I can tell. Hear me out this time, Tory, please."

She tilted her head back, looking up into his face as she struggled to regain her composure. "Well, of course, after . . . I mean, it's the least I can do after you've come all this way . . . to bring Jake."

"Yes, Jake." He cleared his throat, and seemed to be choosing his words carefully. "He's had a tough week, what with the quills and . . . and everything."

"But he's okay now?"

"He's fine, except for missing you, that is."

"I've missed him too."

"That's one of those things I wanted to talk about. When you left, I thought . . . well, actually you *said* . . . that having a dog around wasn't part of your plans."

"But I didn't really mean it. I was having sort of a bad time that day—"

"I guessed as much, once Don told me you sent word for him to ship Jake up here as soon as possible." He hesitated and then continued. "I figured that out, and a few other things, after you left. Jake's not the only one in Silver Pine who's missed you."

"Oh?"

"Amy and Darla and Sarah—"

"And?" She forced the word out, and waited.

"And so have I." He reached out then and grasped her arms, the warmth of his touch sending a shiver all the way down her spine.

It took Tory some time to absorb the words she had been longing to hear. Now that she had heard them, she wanted to curl up and savor the slowly spreading happiness within her. He had missed her. He hadn't been pretending. Through a preoccupied haze, she attempted to comprehend what he was saying.

"Did you hear me, Tory? I missed you too." He spoke seriously, his brow furrowed as he struggled to express his feelings. "Look, I know I have no right to say this, but I'm going to anyway. That other guy, Carson—"

"Carson's just a friend."

Intent on saying what he had come all this way to say, Brian swept on as though he hadn't heard. "Maybe he's the one you want, and we've only known each other a few days, but I can't let you out of my life forever before

I tell you—'' As the significance of her words finally penetrated, he stopped and then asked, ''What are you talking about? You were coming back to Seattle for your engagement party.'' Now Brian seemed to be the one having trouble following the conversation.

''That wasn't . . . ah . . . actually the case.''

''But you said . . . you were so anxious to get away from Silver Pine—''

''Well, that was true enough . . . at the time,'' Tory said. ''There was some confusion involved.''

''There still is. I'm not following this at all.''

''Could I explain later, please? For now, just take it as an irrevocable fact that Carson Finley is a dear, dear friend of mine—and nothing more.''

''Then you're not engaged to him,'' he said.

''Absolutely not.''

''Or to anybody else?''

''That's right.''

''Well, then . . . maybe we should start this conversation over.'' He looked down at her with such intensity that she felt dizzy.

''Maybe instead we could take it up in the middle, with whatever you were just about to tell me,'' Tory suggested, looking up at him with equal intensity.

''We want you back, Tory, all of us—but especially me . . . I want you back. There's been something . . . a current . . . flowing between us ever since we met. I feel it so strongly that you must feel it too.'' He gripped her arms even tighter. ''I never meant to deceive you. It was just . . . bad timing, and that stupid promise to Sarah . . . and then I had to go to Forty-Mile and couldn't get back. Everything got all tangled up.''

Tory moved closer and murmured encouragingly, "Yes, it certainly did."

"And then when Sarah—bless her meddling little heart—called you last week and you told Mike to toss those guys right off your property, well, I knew I'd somehow gotten all the wrong impression about you selling out to California Development. And that day in my office, I really saw red when I thought you were abandoning poor old Jake here." He broke off in disgust at his inability to convey his feelings. "Tory, I'm saying this all wrong."

"No, you're not, Brian. You're doing just fine. To be honest, those mistaken impressions weren't really your fault. I'm embarrassed to admit that I created them on purpose, to punish you for pretending to be interested in me—"

"Pretending? What do you mean, pretending? I did everything but hang by my knees from a tree limb to impress you. Ever since I saw you on the road that first day, sputtering and glaring at me, I knew I wanted to get to know you better."

"You certainly hid it well."

"I thought I was making myself clear the night we walked back from Sarah's after dinner. And you seemed pretty friendly that night too."

"Now that *wasn't* a mistaken impression."

"You weren't all that friendly the day Jake found the porky. I had more quills in me than he did!"

"Poor Brian. You've had a terrible time. Maybe I can make it up to you. Do I seem unfriendly right now?" She asked, moving even closer.

"Not exactly."

"Well, then . . . ?"

"So I guess that means you're not mad at your secretary for letting me in today."

"Marie? She's getting a bonus."

"And the other one, Stacy . . . reminds me of Cindy . . . couldn't keep a smile off her face the whole time she was hiding us till your meeting was done. I was sure she'd blow the surprise. . . ."

"A bonus for her too."

"They were a big help to me. You run a mighty friendly office."

"It seems to be getting friendlier all the time."

"Jake, you're going to have to stand aside," Brian said, gently nudging the dog away from Tory. "I have some important business here." Jake, agreeable as always, walked a few feet away and settled down on the carpet. At last, Brian folded Tory into his arms and kissed her as though he'd never let her go. She wound her arms around his neck and returned the favor.

Sometime later, she vaguely heard the office door open and close quickly, followed by Stacy's whoop of laughter. Apparently, Tory's secretaries had figured out that Ms. Baxter wasn't upset at them for letting the tall stranger and the golden dog into her office—not upset at all.